LIFE IN POCKETS

Chapters.

1. Introduction to Pockets.
2. The perfect painting.
3. Life before.
4. As the years went on.
5. No rest.
6. Brand new pocket.
7. The beginning or the end.
8. Meet Doctor Khan.
9. Still in the shadow.
10. The school meeting.
11. Round two.
12. Meet April.
13. Have I lost?
14. Broken tomb.
15. Show time!
16. The truth.
17. My happyish ending.

CHAPTER 1.
INTRODUCTION TO POCKETS.

Not everything we see is what it seems. You know, the saying, 'Don't judge a book by its cover' and all that shit. We are all guilty of one thing or another. It does not have to be serious or meaningful, nor do we even need to be aware of what it is we are guilty of. It's just still there and always will be, tucked away in the little pockets of life.

These pockets of life are where we humans store all our unnecessary crap that we all insist on carrying around with us inside our tiny minds. I say pockets because everyone has at least two: one for guilt and one for regret. Some people may even have more. Maybe one for memories, or one for achievements. Either way, we all carry some sort of shit around with us that we don't actually need. Although there are many possible reasons for us to acquire these life pockets, the main two we seem to focus on are regret and definitely guilt. I think this is due to how overpowering these feelings are, that we don't really have much energy for the rest.

Now, these pockets, just like any pockets, will eventually get full if we are not careful. The thing is, once they are full can we, or are we able to empty them? Where do we store all the guilt that has built up? Or the tower of regret we have sculpted? It's not like we can do a spring clean and throw away a bag or two of guilt and maybe downsize our tower of regret. We can't... so we keep adding to it. You add to it, they add to it, and even the stranger at the bus stop adds to it. We are all responsible for drip-feeding emotions into each other's pockets. Not always purposely of course. I mean you get the odd idiot that willingly goes out of their way to make someone feel like shit, but not everyone is like that. Have you ever been or had a person so happy to see you while you are out shopping? And you have no clue who they are? Yeah, well you just added a bit of embarrassment and maybe a touch of shame to their pockets, and they repaid you with that stupid feeling mixed with guilt for forgetting them. Well done!

Once our pockets are full and bursting at the seams, they overspill and become harder for us to conceal or hide. They over spill into our hearts and minds, taking control of the person we are, or once were. Once this happens and our hearts and minds start to become overpowered by so many mixed emotions and feelings, we find ourselves standing in the centre of a crossroads. Can we fight this? We could just give up? We also could sit down in the hope someone will come along and pick us up. Or my favourite, just go home to bed and pretend it's not happening.

So, once we had chosen the direction we wanted to head in, surprisingly it was a wrong choice. What then? Our heads have no room to overspill and there is no drip tray for our hearts! All that is left to do is explode! I don't mean physically explode! But more mentally. Scream! Shout! Let it all out! Until we are left with nothing more than a shell of a person. Don't worry though you are going to have some sort of inkling this is due... I mean you are not going to wake up one morning and during the night your mental state has thought 'fuck this' and left. No one is that lucky.

We all must suffer one way or another, just like we all are responsible for contributing to each other's pockets and packing them full of irrelevant bullshit that we all insist on keeping with us throughout our lives. The number of pockets one can keep has no limits. It is the strength and capacity of the pockets that causes the issue. We get the strength from our minds and the capacity from our brains. This doesn't mean if you were unlucky enough to be born with a neurodiverse brain you are more likely to crash sooner. In fact, it's the opposite. Having a neurodiverse brain is a curse but also a gift. A gifted curse if you like. Even though all brains develop similarly, no two brains function the same. A neurodiverse brain works differently from a neurotypical brain. I was blessed with what I like to call a borderline or high-functioning neurodiverse brain. The most dangerous brain of all for life pockets.

No, I am not a brain specialist or doctor, but I know me, and I know how different and weird I am compared to the average person. I know how I am supposed to behave or the mannerism I am supposed to show but my brain will not allow this. Unlike the average person, I am torn between thinking inside the box while seeing the dangers that lie outside the box. I cannot fully speak for neurotypical people, but if I had to guess they drew the long straw. Imagine being able to go out to work or socialise with friends and not feel like you are developing a brain tumour or heading towards a cardiac arrest caused by asphyxiation. It sounds too dangerous if you ask me! Wandering around, in a crowd without a care in the world! No irrational thoughts to keep you safe! This is where the neurodiverse brain becomes a gifted curse. You either have no care in the world or your brain was made to take a beating and endure any punishment that may come our way. I strongly feel that if a neurotypical person's brain was made to feel or think the way a neurodiverse brain would, they would not survive very long.

It does not matter if you have thicker skin than others or are even unlucky enough to be brought into this world with pre-made holes.

Some people may live a happy well protected life whereas others are kicked to the curb. Some are strong minded, and some have more of a sensitive mind. It doesn't matter what skin you have or the life you live, even the strongest of people can crash.

My pockets got full a long time ago and yep you guessed it, I took my favourite road to the land of sleep, in the hope it would all be just a bad dream. But it wasn't! And all I have left of the once happy life is now the dream.

CHAPTER 2.
THE PERFECT PAINTING.

Let's go back a year or two, when life was pretty peachy. It had its soft, sweet, fuzzy moments but it also had its sour, tooth breaking centre. But I wasn't complaining, not much anyway.

Living in a 2-bed semi-detached house with one loving husband Daniel and two little girls Emily and Amelia. They were so beautiful it was as if they came out of a dream. I was content with life. We lived a stereotypical life. The grass was always cut with a border of pretty flowers. Flowers of all colours, painting the picture of happiness. The garden path was as straight as a ruler with a small stepping stone path leading to the driveway. Just before you reached the driveway, we had a pretty round rosebush. Although this added to our perfect family portrait and was such a pretty feature in our garden, them thorns were proper little pricks. A bit like our neighbours, they would not think twice about stabbing you in the leg as you walked past. At least they looked and smelled nice.

Maybe I should elaborate.

We had two sets of neighbours, one on each side of us. They were all like chalk and cheese but both equal arseholes. To the left, in the joining house, we had Mr. and Mrs. Jenner. She was all prim and proper and walked as if she had a stick up her arse whereas he was such a peaceful man. It almost made you think if their marriage was consenting considering he could never get a word in edge ways.

Mrs. Jenner. The perfect lady. I'm sure she must model herself on the queen. With not a hair out of place, she looked down her nose at everyone and was always the first to witness a crisis, or what she thought was a crisis. She also claimed not to be a big drinker but I'm sure she had a tipple of sherry in her morning coffee as a help aid to keep up that stiff posture. It was Mr. Jenner I felt sorry for. He had such a lovely manner about him, always polite and never was one to keep you chatting long. They have both retired now so the poor guy can't even go to work for a break. To the right were the tweeds. They didn't have a stick up their arse, in fact I don't even think they had spines.

Now, the Tweeds. What a different kettle of fish they were. They really did seem to wear their problems on the outside, and without a doubt we all got front row seats. I don't think the Tweeds were actually married. In fact, I am almost certain they weren't. Well, I never heard it, and

Mrs. Jenner hasn't chewed my ear off about it. I really do try my best to hide from Mrs. Jenner the morning after a Tweed party, but she always manages to catch me. Mainly when I am taking out the rubbish. Did you hear them! Did you see what happened! Mavis will be turning in her grave if she knew what a disgraceful mess they have made of her house.

Mavis was Mrs. Jenner's friend. She had originally owned the house the Tweeds now inhabit. I never actually got to meet the famous Mavis as she was taken ill before we got to view our house. Mrs. Jenner really spoke highly of her though and by the sounds of things she looked up to Mavis as if she were her older sister. If I had to guess though, I would have to assume Mavis was the dragon trainer, and the dragon was Mrs. Jenner. Do not get me wrong, she was not at all a vicious dragon but more of a territorial one. No one goes in or out without her knowing! And if something was to upset or disturb the little sleeping dragon then everyone got burnt ears!

I always make sure I take a brew and a cigarette with me now when I take the rubbish out just in case. Mrs. Jenner has this habit of emerging from the privets, slowly and very quietly, like a lion ready to pounce just to chat my ears off about something. I would not even put it past her to try and take a sneaky bite of my leg when my back is turned. Maybe if Mavis was still with us, I would be the one being able to rest in peace.

The Tweeds were loud. And when I say loud, I mean very loud! At everything! and all the time as well. I don't even think they are capable of being quiet, never mind knowing how to monitor their own volume. I am almost positive I can even hear them eating their food as I know I can definitely hear them sleep! And our houses are not even attached!

The Tweeds were very social beings. Always having people around to make as much noise as they possibly could. They really did like to party! Some went on for days! Singing, laughing, fighting, it really was a breeding ground for pocket fillers. They were not very tidy people either. Recreating their weekly shopping list would not be that hard, all you would have to do was look around their garden and make a list of the empty packets, cans or bottles just lying on the ground. Mrs. Jenner actually set up her own petition to try and get the council to evict them. Obviously, it did not make any difference as they are still here.

Their children were no more evolved than their parents. In fact, they are very much carbon copies of them. Just as loud, just as rude! I was just grateful my girls did not get the chance to build any form of relations with them.

Life back then was pretty perfect. It had its normal ups and downs but nothing to complain about, nothing major anyway. It's a shame that now, that pretty picture that painted the perfect family life is now full of darkness, silent screams, and blood splattered memories.

I really should introduce myself.

Hi, I am Samantha Nichols. The once perfect-ish wife, mother, and daughter but the now possible widowed, incarcerated psychopath known as phyco-Sam. A name which I acquired, not purposely, of course. Having any sort of illness is hard but a mental health illness is always a life changer. Not just for us either. Mental illnesses do not just harm the person suffering but everyone connected to that person, whether it be friends or family, partner or child. No one comes out the other side unharmed, well that is if we are strong enough to see the other side.

Life as I know it today isn't all bad. I mean it's far different from my earlier life and very limited, but I can't complain really. I guess I could compare the difference between then and now to Heaven and Hell. The only difference being Is that I am just as content in Hell as I was in Heaven. Strange really, especially when you consider the person I was. A fully functioning human being, capable of creating, building, and nourishing my own little family. Although if I am honest on some days, I am still that person. Not physically of course but my heart, soul and mind are still there along with my sanity. It is only the shell of the person I became that is left here, in this life, and as for my family, well like I said, no one is left unharmed all I can do is hope they are all safe and well!

As you have probably guessed my pockets got full, bursting in fact. A bit like a plastic carrier bag full of shopping that has split, and you are at them crossroads I mentioned earlier.

Do you chase the cabbage?

Or do you follow the beans?

Is this the time to cry over spilt milk?

Or do we just simply lie face down on the ground and scream into a pillow made from a loaf of bread?

Chaos, right?
Chaos with a cherry on!

Well, it would have had a cherry on, but I am fairly sure the cherries have buggered off along with the cabbage and beans.

From that moment to now is an awfully long, exceptionally long story. A story that you would rather be reading than living.

Stories are good though. Whether it is a true story or totally imaginary, a filmed story or a written story, there is something for everyone. When you think about it, every person, creature, even thing, big or small has a story. The only difference being is they do not always have someone to tell it. Even stories created from the imagination are not just plucked from fresh air! The seed must have been planted somehow. Whether something had broken or been fixed, something had been done or undone, seen or unseen. Either way, the seed or seeds have been planted and with a little encouragement are able to grow and blossom into fabulous stories. Now this encouragement that enables the story seeds to grow does not always take the form of cheerleaders, supporting family or a bottle or two of wine, but can nine out of ten times be found in our pockets! Life pockets! The pocket theory!

I know, I know, I sound obsessed with these life pockets but hear me out, I have a theory. A story is told in order to imitate something that has happened, going to happen, or is wished to happen. Therefore, we must have heard, done, seen, or believed in something for the idea AKA seed to be planted in our minds. All it needs then is a little sprinkle of encouragement from one or all our life pockets to get the ball rolling. For example, if I had a horror story seed planted, I would root through my embarrassment pocket for a motive, then maybe either my anger pocket or revenge pocket for a plan, then I would probably scour my greatest fears and possibly my nightmare pocket for the outcome. Boom! I now have a blossoming story. Do not get me wrong though, although we all have these life pockets mostly everyone has their own ways and reason for how they are used.

So, in a nutshell, all our shit can be used to our advantage and turned into something new and spectacular, or something darker and creepier. But let's keep it positive shall we.

I was not always this happy to see the end of life as I know it. In fact from the little I can remember growing up I was quite a pleasant child (although my mum may have had a different story). I do not remember much from when I was very young or have many stories to share. Maybe nothing significant happened or I just needed room to remember grown up shit and forgotten it all. My mum and dad would tell me the odd story about how I would wander off and get lost. Or my dad's favourite! "Remember that time you tried to drink a bottle of fizzy pop while lying down!" Yes dad! Yes, I do! It stuck up my nose for hours! I nearly drowned in my own laziness! Not my proudest moment but like I said, nothing significant happened.

I do remember some of my teen years though. Always wishing I was a grown up. Living in my own house where no one could tell me what to do or what time to do it. I would not have to waste my time washing dishes or doing the shitty jobs my mum used to make me do. And best of all I could eat what I want and get out of bed whenever I felt like it. I really thought I was going to live the life. Oh, how naïve I was! I really do understand now why my mum was constantly muttering,

"You kids don't know how lucky you are," Or, "You should not wish your life away!" Yeah, maybe I should have listened to my mum more but at the end of the day nothing can slow down time, so my life would have gone this quick no matter what I did.

My school life was not all that bad either. I mean I was called the odd name, but nothing sinister. One thing I do miss about the old days was how free my mind felt! How much lighter my pockets were! Every child deserves to be kept free of life pockets and it is the adult's job to carry them, to keep them safe until they are ready to take on life themselves. Well until they at least hit puberty. Puberty is when our pockets start to blossom. At first, when our pockets start to develop, they are as messy as a teenager's bedroom. Nothing is put away in the order it should be. Every problem, issue and upset is just swept up into one big pile and shoved into the nearest pocket. That is why I feel teenagers are always tired, and emotional and feel like the world is out to get them. They are confused. One thing I said a lot as a teenager was, "You will never understand" or "I'm going through hell and you don't care." When in reality, it was me that did not understand and 'going through hell'? Bitch, please! Everything always seemed a million times worse as a teenager. Learning new feelings for the first time and having to take time to self-regulate again.

Let's just start again, this time from the top. The top being when I met Daniel. Daniel and I were noticeably young when we met and no, we did not fall in love with each other at first sight. Well, there was falling but it was not in love.

CHAPTER 3.
LIFE BEFORE.

It was a warm summery night in the middle of May, and I was a young seventeen-year-old lady. I think I had more of a fourteen maybe fifteen-year-old mentality. Being a late bloomer my pockets were only just starting to blossom. There was no fancy teen beach party where the night was young, and no, our eyes did not meet across the glittering sand and our love did not sparkle throughout the night. Nope, quite the opposite in fact. I was a socially awkward teen that lived in the middle of town and was in a stinking mood because my mum sent me out to buy milk. Yes, milk!

Where I lived was not too bad, it was a cul-de-sac off a main road, so it was not that busy in our square. I was able to play out without too much worry from my mum. The only way in was the same way out, so the only traffic we really got was people turning around from going the wrong way.

There were two more children that lived in our square, Jessica, and her brother Ralph. Everyone else was old and had lived there years. Jessica and Ralph were both younger than me. Jessica was around two years younger and her brother three, maybe four. Now in adult years two years age difference is nothing but as a kid, two years is like ten adult years. When I was in high school, Jessica was not even in her last year of primary school! I definitely thought I was too old and wise to hang around with primary school children. Shame Jessica never saw it that way. Always knocking on my door asking, "Is Sam playing out." If I did not make it to the door before my mum, I would have to pretend I was doing homework or else I would have to listen to the lecture about how she was a nice girl that only wanted to be my friend. Yeah well, she had no choice but to want to be my friend due to lack of options! It was not my fault she was not allowed out of the square. On the occasions I was unsuccessful and was forced out of my own home, I would just stand there, arms crossed and leaning on my wall until at least ten minutes had passed. I thought that was a reasonable amount of my time spent outside with Jessica. Thinking back now, she was not all bad and was a genuinely nice girl. Well-mannered but very talkative. But, me being an only child going through teenage stuff, I was just not in the mood for 'talkative'.

Jessica's brother, Ralph was rarely seen outside. In fact, I only saw him going to and from his mum's car. Not sure what his issues were but my mum

said he was not as fortunate as us. I never fully
understood what my mum was trying to say until
I got older, but to me he seemed to have the ideal
life. Not having to go out or walk anywhere. I am
not going to lie I was a tiny bit jealous. Once I met
Daniel, I never really saw them much after that,
but I heard Ralph committed suicide at twenty-
five years old. As for Jessica, well last I heard
she was drinking herself into an early grave. It
was a little bit like the ugly duckling story read
backwards. I am quite fortunate in that aspect of
my life as I have never really had to deal with a
death so close to my heart. Losing a sibling in that
way really must have been a pocket burster.

Having a person there all of those years then
suddenly they're gone, is something my mind
cannot make sense of. Don't get me wrong I
fully understand how death works and that it is
inevitable, but the memories and the pictures
in my mind cannot. Take a chicken dinner for
instance. If you were served a chicken dinner
without the chicken, it's still a dinner and, in your
mind, you can imagine the chicken there, where
it is supposed to be. You eat it because you must,
but it will never be the same without the chicken.
But eventually that dinner without chicken will
become the norm and the chicken is then not
missed, and that is what my mind will not come to
terms with. I don't want a dinner without chicken
just like I do not want my life without my mum or

dad.

It was a warm May day and I was stomping to the supermarket for milk. I was never a real girly girl, so my wardrobe consisted of many oversized t-shirts, shorts and jeans and as it was warm I set off on my journey in an oversized t shirt, shorts and flipflops. Now many ladies would know that walking while in a mood with flipflops on is just like adding salt to a wound. There are so many different outcomes for this journey to end. I mean I could make it to the shop safe, get the milk safe and then make it home happy enough to live happy ever after. But this was me and I never have been the one to take the easy way out.

As I steamed down the road like an unoiled steam train, I fell right through the supermarket doors. And yes, you read right, I fell. Not a little slip that I could easily walk off and escape with only a hand full of embarrassment and maybe a pulled leg muscle because that would be too easy. I went for gold! Full belly flop on the entrance mat of the supermarket, right next to the security guards post and in front of the self-checkout tills.

While I lay there for what was two seconds, but felt like hours, I had just enough time to hatch my come back plan. Plan one was to play dead! But that would have drawn a bigger crowd, which I really did not need at this point. Plan two, claim I was knocked over by a running shoplifter! After consideration I came to the obvious conclusion that for this plan to work I really should not have fallen in front of the security guy with his camera for proof. The final plan was to stand up, shout, "For fuck's sake, there should be a sign there" and then gracefully stomp off as if this was not at all my fault but the fault of the store. Master plan! I chose that one.

My master plan seemed to work, and I eventually made it safely to the fridges where the milk was kept. As I reached for the fridge door, I hear a voice say, "The floor is wet so please don't fall, again." The person then let out a small chuckle. Oh, I was already in the worse mood possible at this point, so I grabbed my milk, slammed the fridge door and turned around faster than my mum did when you dropped one of her favourite plates. I lifted the milk above my head in mid turn in order to show the chuckling voice my rage once I had completed my anger spin. Yeah, that failed, miserably. I was let down by the flipflop! By this point I had rose so high and fell even lower. At least the milk was safe, somehow, I still had it held above my head. Instead of the milk being a threatening weapon, it became a trophy. One that I held high and took pride in the fact that it was saved, and things could have been worse. Imagine having to walk home covered in milk in the warm weather! Ew! Flakes of crusty milk falling off me as I hobble, all stinky with only one flipflop home. I definitely dodged a bullet on that one.

Well by this time I had already given up. Leaving all feeling on the floor in a chalked outline of a Jane Doe, I just stood up. Once up I was able to put a face to the voice that had pretty much nearly finished me off. Dark hair, brown eyes, not a bad looking face either, but nevertheless I had to try and keep up my moody-no-shits-given teenage front. I stood up, proudly held the milk out in front of me and said, "So? I saved the milk didn't I." Immediately I died a little more inside.

In response, the rude but good-looking human laughed. That's right, he laughed. Laughed right in my face! Well, it was not directly in my face but considering how I like to be left alone, anyone that makes it into my view is invading my space. At this point I think I was suffering from a short burst of shock. I no longer felt any anger but my embarrassment had fallen to the bottom of my pocket. As I looked at his laughing face I couldn't help but join in. It was a genuine laugh. I did not even think I was capable of laughing. Well after realising I actually snort when I laugh, I decided to yell, "My name is Sam," before hobbling off with my one flipflop, holding onto my milk and praying I made it home as quickly and safely as possible.

From that day onwards I never minded going to the supermarket for milk. Well, I never minded going for milk any afternoon except weekends! In fact, I may have even started to drink more milk! You know, because it is good for your bones!

Everyone wants stronger bones!

After a few weeks of walking around the supermarket happily buying milk, I got to know the rude, laughing, dark haired human. His name was Daniel. He only worked there part time and as you guessed, his work hours were every afternoon, except weekends. This became a turning point in my life as for the first time I actually cared what someone thought of me, so I started to take more pride in my appearance. I tried to wear nicer clothes and present myself better along with better footwear! I did not go full crazy on my new look, just a few subtle but needed changes. Like less baggy tops, I started to put my hair up nicer instead of leaving it down and flapping about like an injured bird. I did try experimenting with a little make up but that didn't go over so well.

I am not sure how long it was before I got to see Daniel outside of the supermarket, I just know it was a good while. Oh and of course it was awkward! My mum had decided to get me a weekend job. She said it would be good for me. Plus, her friend worked there and was complaining over tea and biscuits about how they need more weekend workers. So, my mum being the mum she was, volunteered my services. Apparently, I had nothing better to do and there was no better time to learn the hardship of working life then now.

It was not a flashy job but a job all the same. I was only re-stacking and organizing rails in a clothes shop. Pretty straight forward. The uniform I had to wear was the hardest part! Oh, it was horrible! I guess it did match the theme of the clothes shop I worked in. It was for, shall we say, the older generation. It consisted of a light blue and white polka dotted blouse. Blouse! And an ankle length matching skirt. I was a young, hip, teenage girl! I did not need this in my life! It was itchy! Sweaty! And smelt like dust! Honestly, I could of taken it home to wash but I had a seventeen-year-old reputation to uphold. No way was I being seen carrying that thing home.

This uniform was so bad it introduced me to anxiety! In fact, I am sure the label read 'made with 100% recycled anxiety'. The thought alone makes me shiver!

So, the day I finally saw Daniel outside of the supermarket, the day started like any other. I got up late, missed breakfast, nearly died running for the bus, got to work, listened to my mum's friend tell me how I was "not taking the job seriously" and "what would your mum say". I had switched off by this point and before I knew it, I was standing, folding up knitted jumpers to make nice fancy piles for people to see.

I must have forgotten to switch myself back on as my guard was that low, someone was able to creep up behind me, grab my waist as they shouted,

"Boo!" Before I had chance to acknowledge who this person was, I had already spun 180 degrees with fists at the ready.

"Oh, it's you," I blurted out with a little nervous giggle that followed. It was Daniel in all his glory. A lucky Daniel at that. I could have punched him in the face. I do sometime wonder where we both would be now if I did punch him square on in the face. Would he still have married me? Maybe! Maybe not! It could have saved us from the mess we were in now! Or it could have been worse.

Still in shock, my head was overloading as a million things ran through my head all at once. The first thing that ran through my head was 'what the fuck is he doing here' and the last was 'I am dressed like a 90s school secretary'. I felt like dropping to my knees, crawling under a rack of clothes and dying.

"Awe! Look at your little outfit," Daniel said as he swished my skirt with his hand.

"Yeah, well, look at your face!" I said before turning back around in utter shame. What the fuck was wrong with me. Idiot.

I am not sure if it was the things I said that Daniel found funny, or the fact I clearly kick myself every time I open my stupid mouth. Whichever one it was he laughed and said, "You know you love me really!" He then walked away. I'm not going to lie, I was shocked. Happy but shocked. No one had ever gone out their way to give me attention before.

For the rest of that day, I was left feeling odd inside. He was so annoying but yet made me feel so much better. He seemed to be embracing my weirdness! Maybe he was broken? I just found it hard to believe that anyone would enjoy being around me unless there was something wrong with them. Do two wrongs make a right? Fuck knows! All I know is that day triggered something inside me which led me to start avoiding Daniel.

Seeing Daniel that day at work added a whole bucket full of embarrassment to my pocket as well as stitching me a brand-new pocket for relationships. Still to this day I have no idea why I felt so nervous that I felt the need to avoid him. I clearly liked him and thought of nothing else, but the anxiety of seeing him again after that day really scared me. What if he was actually making fun of me and I got hit by the wrong end of the stick! I must have only managed maybe another two weekends at the job before I quit, it was just not a place I felt I belonged.

After what felt like a lifetime of avoiding Daniel, my mum finally made me go to buy milk. I must have changed my clothes a million times before my mum got sick of waiting and finally kicked me out the house. I was so nervous that I felt sick. I needed a plan of action.

As the supermarket got closer, the only plan I

could come up with was to sneak in, grab the milk, then out, stealth style!

As the supermarket doors opened, I made sure to scan the shop floor for Daniel before I entered. With no sighting of him, I quickly rushed to the fridge and grabbed the milk. So far so good! I even managed to get to the till and pay for the milk safely without seeing him. All was good until out of nowhere I started to feel crappy. It was as if I was gutted, I did not bump into him, and I was a little offended that he was not here. Could I have secretly wanted to see him? I know what I felt, avoidance, so why was I now feeling disappointed? What if he was here and is avoiding me? Well that would be rude! Maybe he had found his one true love, that was not me. The nervous feeling suddenly changed to pure disappointment as I left the supermarket with my milk.

As I sulkily made my way to the car park wishing I was a different person entirely, I heard his voice.

"Are you not going to say hi?" he shouted as he pushed a long line of trolleys back into their bay. As much as I hate to admit it, I was happy to see him. We stood and talked for a while about why he was sent outside to work.

Then he mentioned that he had not seen me for a while, which I replied with, "Awe did you miss me?"

"Yeah," he said simply. At this point I may have

looked cool as ice on the outside, but inside I was freaking the fuck out! I was not used to this kind of attention, especially someone liking me.

Eventually Daniel said he better get back to work before he is told off for dossing. I awkwardly lifted my hand to say bye before turning in the direction of my house and started to walk off thinking how stupid I must look right now. I had not walked three steps before Daniel shouted, "If you give me your phone number, you won't have to make up excuses to come and see me." He then started to laugh.

I really was so far away from my comfort zone, I just shouted back, "Here then." He took his phone out of his pocket, typed in my number then gave me a one ringer so I could save his.

Walking home was loads easier than walking there. I felt lighter, happier but still nervous. A good nervous, I think! Well, that was until my brain recovered from the shock. What if he didn't text me? Am I supposed to text him first? What would I say? Why does everything have to be so hard. Daniel did text me that evening and I did text him back. We started to talk all the time after that and even started to meet up after work.

CHAPTER 4.
<u>AS THE YEARS WENT ON.</u>

As the years went on, the life me and Daniel started together grew. It was a good few years from the day we met until we were in the position to buy our first proper home together. Daniel had left the supermarket after he had finished his business studies. He managed to get a job at an energy connections company as an administrator.

We visited and viewed so many houses before we decided on ours. Daniel was as finicky as me, so it took longer than we thought as it needed to not only look right but the feeling needed to be right. House after house, day after day, the daunting thought of house hunting was becoming exhausting. I started to believe we were doomed to settle for less and our dream home was a nonsensical thought. One house we looked at did not even have kitchen cupboards. Maybe they mixed up the listing information, instead of 'needs improvements' it should have been 'needs demolishing'. The house we settled on was not perfect, but it did have a warm and welcoming feeling, plus kitchen cupboards.

During the viewing of our house, we were lucky enough to meet Mrs. Jenner. I thought she was the estate agent until the actual one came to introduce herself. She even apologized for Mrs. Jenner's behaviour saying she had been at it all day. Nosey cow would still be at it in her grave no doubt. As for the Tweeds it was at least six months before we met them. The house they were to move into was still owned by Mavis. I think by the time we had moved in, Mavis had been taken ill and spent her remaining time in hospital. Although we never actually got to meet her, we got to hear about her all the time.

After a year or two of settling in our new home we got married. Never in a million years did I think I would end up married. In fact, it had just never appealed to me. People always talk about how their wedding day was the best day of their lives or make it out as if every girl dream of such a magical day. Surely I am not the only girl in the world that feels being the centre of attention is the worst place to be? I always imagined having a wedding would be just as nerve wrecking as standing in front of an army of people waiting to be executed. The run up is long winded, plus the build-up of anxiety was immense. If a choice was given, I would have chosen the execution. At least with an execution I knew the end was near. In all honesty our wedding day was not as bad as I had dreamt. It was short, sweet and over pretty quickly. I think the anxiety of planning, then waiting was the drainer. We just opted for a nice quiet registry office with no fancy-dancy-shite.

After the service we had a little get-together at Daniel's parents' house. His parents were social people and his mum, Irene, just loved making buffets and catering for people. Daniel's dad, Andrew, was a funny guy, just like him always joking around. They both were very different from my parents. Mine never really did much apart from work and take care of me. Although both parents seemed to get on with each other, it was still best to keep their contact at a minimum. Both my parents were work orientated and took a lot more things seriously than his parents would. His parents lived for the moment, whereas mine lived for a secure future.

My mum, Sarah, was a very clean, organised person who was always open and honest, brutally sometimes. My dad, Jack, was a well-dressed hard-working man. Eat, sleep and repeat, he used to always say.

Although Daniel had the fun, go lucky parents, I loved mine. They were perfect to me. I may not have shown it much growing up and could have possibly been an arsehole some of the time. Plus, Daniel had two older brothers to share with growing up, Jake and Sebastian. I was an only child with only myself to share with. That's probably why I assumed the world evolved around me.

As I think back, I am not sure if we had a proper honeymoon. We did stay in a caravan park for a long weekend not long after the wedding, does that count? It was not too far of a distance from where we lived, maybe an hour or hour and a half drive. It was nice though.

Not much was to really change after that until I gave birth to our first daughter, Emily. The pregnancy was not at all like you see on the tele, especially the adverts. Paint adverts are the worst! One happy couple hugging and smiling while they look around at their freshly painted baby's room! It was more like, one crying mum with a don't you dare touch me attitude, with one tired dad that would rather be somewhere else. Both staring at an undecorated room full of crap that has never been unpacked from when we moved in. Basically the room was like that drawer everyone has that they use to dump random shit in.

Like I said my pregnancy was not at all happy and I looked more gloomy than blooming. My first-time mother's aura was more of a devil's shadow. Why the fuck I put myself through it a second time was beyond me. I definitely got some weight in my pockets during those times. I remember this one time, I really needed the toilet and was in the corner shop. The shop assistant was more interested in her phone than my urinary needs. I asked if there was a toilet I could use which she replied, "It's only for staff." I nicely explained my situation but to be honest it was not a secret, I was clearly pregnant and needed a wee. She then said, "Are you staff? No! Now have a nice day!"

Well, by this point I had a full bladder, a practically fully grown child plus a lot of anger to hold in. I had to let something out, so I uncrossed my legs and peed. Yep! I stood there, in the shop, pissed myself, looked at the shop assistants shocked face and said, "Have a nice day." I smiled and left. I felt like a winner walking out that shop door, until the cold hit my wet patch.

Giving birth was not fun at all. I had not really prepared for it either. Constant pain, machines beeping, a nurse in and out my room as if she was on a bungee rope and Daniel being all nice and supportive. Trust me when I say, the last thing you need when you're in pain is a smiling face asking how you are. I mean it is nice but why ask when they can clearly see how I am. I'm fat, in the worst pain of my life trying to squeeze a small human out of my lady garden. To make matters worse, the nurse kept asking me if I would like to go in the birthing pool and I eventually had to say yes just to shut her up. I quickly regretted saying yes. I went into this room that had what looked like a massive paddling pool full of water. The nurse then told me to get undressed and get in. It will be relaxing she said. We have established that I do not crave attention and the thought of being naked, in a massive paddling pool while people stood around looking at me was hell. I am sure it may help some people, but it was not for me, neither was bouncing on that big fricking exercise ball. The only thing I was concentrating on was being able to squeeze out a baby without pooping! I had heard loads of stories from people telling me how they had pooped while pushing, and that was something I was petrified of doing! I know this is coming from the girl who pissed her pants in a shop, but pooping is different! I will say now though, that by the time my second daughter was due, pooping anywhere would have been a bonus.

After eleven gruelling hours of labour, we finally got to meet Emily, weighing 7lb8oz. S eeing Emily's face for the first time was such a powerful feeling, it had a whole life pocket for itself. She was so fragile and just so beautiful I had a mixed feeling of being proud but also scared. My tummy on the other hand just felt empty. I know it was technically emptied when I gave birth, but it felt more than that. It was as if I had no muscles or any internal organs at all. It really was a very odd feeling. Not odd enough to make me miss my baby bump though. I could never really understand why people would say oh just wait, you will miss your bump when its gone. Erm why would I miss not being able to wash my own hair? Or shave my own legs? Or not being able to wash up without having a belly in the sink? I definitely do not miss any of that.

Arriving home with Emily was a proud moment for us as a brand-new family. Of course, Mrs. Jenner was in the garden ready and waiting. She had brought her a little knitted hat with a frill around the edge, a bonnet I think she called it. It was a very nice gift do not get me wrong, it was just I was not the woollen knitted type. I think it must be trauma based from folding all them knitted jumpers at that weekend job I had.

The next few days were busy. People were visiting, all wanting to have a peek at the brand-new family member. I was still trying to get the hang of being a mum, so I did not have much time to make a fool of myself. Well, if I did, I did not care or notice.

Once the busy days had ended and night-time was upon us, I was left with plenty of time to try and soak in all that has happened. The thought of having this little defenceless baby at home was daunting. That cute bundle of flesh and bone was relying on me to survive. To eat, drink and clean. One wrong decision and disaster could strike.

The night-time was proving harder than the days for me. It had nothing to do with being woken up all hours by a crying baby because she was good in that way. It was the fear of not being woken up by a baby that scared me. I used to get so frightened that something may happen to her while I was too busy sleeping that I would try my best to stay awake. What if she stopped breathing? Or a blanket covered her face? She could choke! I loved her so much I could not risk anything happening to her. No wonder my mum only had me, this was stressful.

A week or two later the midwife stopped coming to visit, this meant I had to take Emily to the local clinic to be measured and weighed by her health visitor. Emily always seemed to maintain a nice healthy weight, but I still had to keep her records up to date. I hated that place. It was full of mums chatting together with naked babies on their laps just waiting to be placed on that freezing cold scale to be weighed, poor little things. At least it was only once a week. I did walk around proud though. Pushing my beautiful baby girl in her pram. I even started to feel like a proper adult while I was hanging out all her little outfits on the washing line.

Some days were easier than others and some days got hard. Watching the news on tele could easily trigger a hard day. Hearing storys of the poor, innocent children being hurt or having their tiny lives cut drastically short by the people they rely on and love used to affect me badly. How could something so helpless and precious make you so angry you could physically hurt them! Just thinking of Emily being hurt or suffering made me cry. Just the way she looks at me with need and love melted my heart. It was not long before I had developed a little OCD. Frantically ensuring there were no hazards around my home, constantly making sure she was breathing during the night. I had gotten so overprotective I used to go into full panic mode if Daniel or our parents even thought about taking Emily for a walk. My life had become dedicated to keeping her safe.

Emily was around two years old when I fell pregnant with my second daughter, Amelia. Although both girls were planned, Amelia was more of a ploy to add more meaning to our life and to give company to Emily. I know it sounds selfish when you say it out loud, but everyone has their reasons for having children. Either way the distraction from life was there and worked well for a while. I was once again kept busy with another bundle of joy.

There was no doubt in my mind that I loved and would do anything I possibly could to keep the girls safe and happy, even if I have two extra life pockets to fill.

CHAPTER 5.
NO REST.

I have always been finicky about life. I am just never happy and always at war with my head about something or other. Whether it is because of something that happened today, yesterday or five years ago, I am always in battle. Silently, of course. The worst battles are during the night-time. Every night without any fails, on the tenth second my head hits my pillow to sleep, my mind decides to declare war. Before I know it, I have gone from getting ready to fall asleep to hating the idiot that bumped into me in town three years ago. He really needed to feel the wrath of my anger, as I imagined the moment over, and over again, with each scenario ending differently. These endings had a varied scale of some kind of physical violence, ranging from a simple kick to me being clung to his leg with my teeth, like a little piranha puppy. The incident itself was not at all major but the fact he bumped into me, grunted then walked off without a word, really pissed me off.

It is strange how our minds can take one small incident and allow it to escalate into something much more than it originally was. I often wonder if he or anyone else we think of ever gets a weird feeling randomly and they are unsure of why or what the cause is. Well, if that's so, then it's me. Me, imagining that I have pinned you down on the floor, with your arm seconds from snapping until you apologise. I am not fully sure which of his life pockets our little encounter falls into or even if the event was too insignificant to even land in a pocket. He could have had a family emergency and been unable to stop, and now he has a little extra guilt in his pocket for not apologising. Although sound does travel faster than we can walk so he did not actually need to stop, just talk louder. Maybe he was unable to sleep that night and eventually slotted me into the 'fuck it' pocket and moved on to the next victim of his rudeness. Either way he had managed to sprinkle his existence over many of my pockets. Unknowingly adding his stupid face to my memories and keeping me up all night, which was worse because not only was I pissed off but now I was also tired. And that folks is how hate is conceived.

Hate is not only a powerful feeling but also a powerful word. With hate comes power. And the only thing more hazardous than power is hateful power. Power plus hate always equals war. Sadly, whether the war is with yourself or with a country, it never changes, it just hurts. Shouting I hate you to someone can cut deeper than a knife, especially if that person loves you. We as humans can heal from wounds caused by inanimate objects but seem to struggle to heal from a few simple words. I feel this is because once a physical wound has healed all we are left with is the memory, which is basically a picture in our minds with no feeling. Whereas words cut internally so every time we remember someone saying 'I hate you; or anything else that may have upset us is like picking the scab of a cut and making it bleed. You cannot fix what you cannot see any more than you can take back words spoken.

As you have probably guessed I am a hoarder of feelings. I love nothing more than to store up every little piece of guilt, anger and stupidness without letting any go to waste. This becomes a huge problem for people like me, as the bigger my problems pockets became the more it overpowers my happy pockets and are easily shaken to the top. A bit like lumpy sugar. No matter who you are, if you were to give that nice, sweet sugar a wobble or shake ,all of them lumpy bits will rise to the top like legendary kings. Whether it has one lump or two, you know that sugar is heading for the bin.

I have endured many sleepless nights in my time on this planet. Some bigger than others and some for no reason known. I feel I am a settled non sleeper, if there was such a thing. Take Daniel for instance, he is what I like to call a night walker. If he is not asleep within ten minutes of being in bed, he is up pacing the house as if he is searching for lost treasure. I very rarely get out of bed during the night. I mean I may have the odd bathroom break, but I mainly lay in silence dwelling on irrelevant bullshit.

Lack of sleep doesn't help either! Even well rested people get tired. Being physically tired leaves your body lacking the energy and motivation to move. This encourages your body to become stationary giving your mind the opportunity to slip in and out of daydream mode, which isn't a bad thing. Many good, brilliant things are thought up through daydreaming, but well rested or boredom daydreams differ from exhausted daydreams. Tired induced daydreams consist more of problems or stresses that our rested mind would normally block. Like anything we need to be fully charged in order to function correctly. It is a little bit like our bodies switch onto stand by mode, still using energy, still connected to the WIFI, the only difference being is no one appears to be home.

Don't get me wrong, I am not for one second insinuating that any mental health issue can be fixed by a good sleep or healthy diet. Yeah, it may help a little and even throwing a few pills in there may get you by daily, but it is only a mask. If you are unlucky enough to be held in the grasping hands of any mental illness, running away or hiding only prolongs the inevitable. The battle is real! Young or old, strong minded or weak, boy or girl, mental health does not discriminate or hold back. The tricky part of all this is the recognition. There is no high temperature or rash to look out for. Not even a tickly cough. Even the person suffering may not be able to detect that something was wrong. Our minds become the puppeteer for our bodies, controlling all of our movements so whether mental illness affects us a little or a lot, it is still in control and does not want to be caught.

I am what Daniel liked to call 'my own worst enemy'. Always worrying about crap that I refuse to let go off. It's a hard job to maintain. A hard job that has refused to accept my resignation. I know I'm not helping myself but honestly, most of the time I don't feel like I can. Taking a person's legs then asking them to walk is no different than asking someone with a mental illness to think straight. I do understand how some people may think it is as simple as saying a few positive words to help you feel better, but honestly would we tell someone to grow new legs so you can walk? So why would some positive words fix our broken brains.

Night times for me are the worst. There are so

many hours to just lie-down and think, but not enough hours to sleep. Then I'm getting stressed at the fact I should be asleep, but I am not. Clock watching in hopes that I can manage to slow down time enough to save some precious minutes for sleep. It never works though. In fact, I am pretty sure I have secret power naps in between thoughts. Why else would it take me twenty minutes to blink.

Nights like these became more frequent. Instead of looking forward to jumping into bed after a hard day's graft, I found myself dreading it. The thought of the night ahead churned my stomach, causing knots so painful I would often feel like vomiting. Things for me were clearly taking a turn for the worst as my body and mind became so exhausted, I was left with no other choice. I had to face the fact that I maybe loosing control.

So, my pockets had overflown, and my head had exploded and as predicted I lay my little full head down to sleep through it. Insomnia had set in and all I could imagine was me, standing on the wrong side of a bridge. My mind seemed so clear as I contemplate about taking that leap of faith. How free I would feel as I fell through the air, with my arms spread like a bird bracing myself for the last thing I hoped to ever feel, the ground.

Sleep was no longer on my side so all I had left was to daydream. As I lay daydreaming that I had finally hit the ground after soaring through the air to freedom, the good I am finally free feeling soon faded. As I imagined my lifeless body barely underneath the bridge I fell from, I saw my family. I was beginning to think my own daydreams were now against me. Watching my own family literally picking up my pieces, while the devastation leaked from my body and into the pockets of everyone nearby really made me evaluate my exit from this world. Maybe plummeting to my death was not the best way to leave my mark on this world. Just a stain on the roadside being washed away by the poor suffering souls I had left behind.

It was not long before the numbness set in. Numb from sense or feeling I became withdrawn from life. Just sitting there, staring at life pass me by. Watching the world move without me. The only thing I could hear by this point was my very own self-consciousness. As the days passed me by, the conversations between me and my self, became more frequent.

They were not exciting nor were they fancy conversations. They were more of playground banter than anything. It really was like I was standing in the middle of a playground trying to decide which of the two friends I was going to play with today. The goody two shoes who is always looking out for others or the hard done by friend who feels the world owes them everything. It may sound like there was an obvious choice here, and honestly if my mind was in a good place, I would have been able to choose. But seeing as I felt my head was in no place, good or bad I felt no other choice then to add to my confusion and listen to both.

I was a nice person, at least I think I was. Well I wanted to be nice, but I was also hurting and confused. I felt surrounded by happy people going about their day like they have empty pockets. The hard done by voice inside my mind knows fine well no fucker has empty pockets and hated the fact they are not stuck like me! While the goodie two shoes voice thought it was a good thing, not everyone should suffer just because I am. I often spent hours flicking between both voices like I was playing a tennis match and sadly I feel my hard done by side is winning the match.

"Just look at them all, living! Smiling! Laughing!"

"What are they laughing at?"

"Why are they so happy?"

"Me? It is Me, isn't it? They are laughing at me!"

With every day that passed my hate pocket got that little bit bigger. Every innocent person that made their way past my home contributed to my pocket. My conscious made sure of that. Once my hate pocket got full it started to slowly nibble away at my soul like a family of hungry rats around a loaf of bread. It was only a matter of time now before the last crumb of my soul was ingested and the rats sought food elsewhere.

As I continued my journey into nothingness, all I could do was sit. Just sitting like some creepy doll on a chair, without a word spoken for days, maybe weeks. Although by this point, I became physically unfit for life, my mentality was still there, and I was at its mercy. My subconscious had my undivided attention leaving me to grapple between emotions with an internal monologue. The most heart-breaking thing about getting to this stage with my mental health was that I forgot I was a mother or a wife. My poor girls had no mummy, Daniel had lost not only his wife but best friend too. Both my parents and Daniel's mum helped with the girls when they could, but if I am totally honest, I don't think I even gave anyone a thought, not even my girls. All I could think about was how much I hated everything. I would often replay every situation from my embarrassment pocket in my head, thinking how stupid I was. Why the hell did I not just shut up! Or walk away! Why could I have not been a normal person! I even started to hate people for being able to get on with their daily lives, because I felt like I never could. Imagine being able to get up in the morning and go to work without a panic attack or needing the toilet fifty million times or arranging a night out with friends without coming down with any excuse to cancel.

As my world may appear silent from the outside, inside became louder and darker. All thoughts became destructive beings protesting their way to freedom. It would only be a matter of time before these feelings made their way out. Before any seepage was enabled, every part of my internal body developed their own individual personalities. It was a bit like them cartoons you see with a devil on one shoulder and an angel on the other, the difference being is that I was the animator. An animator who had lost control of what my own mind had created. With the burden of my creations, I could only wish for peace. None stop head chatter was driving me more and more into the dark pit of despair, it wouldn't be long before I broke, properly broke. One can only imagine the mess a full bucket of shit would make with even the slightest of cracks.

With every laughing voice came a crying voice, while one would hate the other shown compassion. The only thing my voices had in common was they never shut the fuck up.

CHAPTER 6.
BRAND NEW POCKET.

During some point in July my internal cracks started to surface. I gained a brand-new pocket, paranoia. The feeling drove through my body like poison. Starting from the tips of my fingers and toes the fire of paranoia spread to my heart like a lethal injection.

This day in particular started as any other. I got out of bed, dragged my carcass down the stairs and parked myself on my chair where I switched to creepy doll mode. The morning was going pretty much like clockwork. Daniel came downstairs around an hour after me, he got the girls ready for school. One of Emily's friends' mums had started to pick up the girls and take them to school every morning since I got poorly. Janet, the mum was called. So around eight thirty I would see the car pull up outside my house and beep. Daniel would peep his head around the curtain, hold up his hand, then Janet will do a little wave from her car. I am pretty sure something was wrong with that woman. Always happy! No real person is that happy every morning. As I sit watching my girls wave bye to Daniel as they jump into Janet's car, I could not help but wonder. Why the fuck is she so happy? It was nothing new, I always looked and tried to figure out her secret, it was just this specific morning I had developed paranoia. Paranoia that just needed a jump start to get going. I continued to observe Daniel's sad face as they look towards the house, talking about me no doubt! Then as always Janet would put her hand on Daniels's shoulder as a sign of comfort, then they would part ways. The only difference was, this morning as Janet put her hand on Daniel's shoulder, I felt a sharp pain in my heart, as if I had just been shot. What the fuck! Why the fucking hell is she touching my husband. Does she not have her own. No wonder the bitch is so happy to pick up my kids.

As the rage sizzled inside my chest, Daniel made his way back into the house. He came into the sitting room and knelt next to me asking me how I was feeling. Then after a minute silence said, "I will make us a coffee, shall I?" He then put his hand on my shoulder. The moment his hand touched my shoulder something inside me woke up. I turned my head for the first time in so long, I looked my husband in the face. His beautiful, caring face was at hands reach. I love him so much, I thought to myself. I fought so hard with myself just to try and lift my arm to touch his face. I never managed to even flinch, I just turned my head back around to continue staring out the window. Daniel silently got to his feet and made his way into the kitchen to make coffee.

After a tiresome day of sitting and staring, as always Daniel would sort the girl's tea and put them to bed. Then he would take my hand and say, "Let's go and get some rest, shall we?." I would then stand and follow Daniel upstairs to our bedroom. My night times were just as exciting as my days, I was just lying down instead of sat on that chair. I could not tell you if or when I had any sleep, and if I did sleep it was no different or quieter than being awake. As I lay thinking, trying to sort through all the chatter I realised that today something inside me had changed. I had a moment where I had actually noticed things as if I was more awake. I feel like I saw Daniel for the first time ever today and that made me smile. I also remembered noticing Janet! Fucking Janet! With her stupid, smiling face and grubby hands touching my husband. I hope she chokes on her cornflakes.

Once both girls were asleep, Daniel went to do all the last checks. I could hear him check the front and back door, he then came upstairs and went into the girl's room to check them. Before he turned off his bedside lamp, he lent over, kissed me on the forehead and said good night. Such a nice moment that should have filled me with love and security, but it had the opposite effect. I was not allowed to feel such feeling so instead as Daniel switched off his lamp, he switched on my internal voices. It was definitely going to be a busy night, and something tells me Janet, is tonight's topic.

Stupid Janet.

Who does she think she is? With all her touching and smiling.

Why is she so fucking happy? All she is doing is picking up someone else's children.

Maybe her family is broken and that's why she must find a better family!

What is actually stopping her from taking my family? Well it's not me, I couldn't even stop Daniel from making coffee earlier.

Whatever her reason for stalling maybe, she is not taking my family! Over my dead body!

Over my dead body? Maybe that's what she is waiting for? Me to curl up and die or kill myself. So, she can just step over me as if I was not there! Well, I am not going anywhere! And If I was to die, I hope she falls over my dead body, smashing her head so hard, she cannot remember what the fuck she was stepping over.

Like I said, long night.

Morning has finally arrived. Another day being stuck in my own head. As always, I got up before Daniel, and parked my butt on my chair, only this time I was waiting. Yeah Janet, I was waiting. Waiting to observe your vicious plan to take away the one thing I did good in my miserable life. With a quick fast forward, the girls were waving bye to Daniel as they jumped in Janet's car. Now was the time to switch to surveillance mode. I had never been the best at lip reading people, but my head was not bad at providing a running commentary. So, this is basically what my head said happened.

Janet spoke in her stupid squeaky voice, "Oh Daniel, I love you so much, I just want to touch your arm, and steal your family."

Then in his man voice Daniel said, "Oh although my wife is watching, I won't stop you from carrying out your evil plan, here I will even willingly give you, my children! Mwahahaha!"

Janet then touched Daniel's shoulder and said, "Let's kill Sam, together." Daniel agreed, and they then went their separate ways.

I had to literally sit for an hour or two to process what my head has just said. Daniel would never hurt me! Or would he? No, he loves me, he cares for me. Or is he trying to lull me into a false sense of security, then BANG he knocks my lights out! Well, I have news for you pal! My lights are fuelled by hate! And you know what they say about hate, don't you?

As it was Friday today the girls got picked up from school by Daniel's mum. Although I think

the girls preferred to stay home, she loved having
them and would often have them for the weekend.
As the evening went on, I had managed to think
of every possible scenario for my death. I even
thought outside the box, with help from my head
friends of course. I was able to act out every scene
individually, in my mind, from start to finish,
as if it was real. Well, we know it is going to be a
premeditated murder, so thought must go into it.
But what kind of murderers could they be? And
how much thought are they able to put into my
slaying? I really need to be ready for anything,
especially ready to karate chop that bitch right
in the throat! Thinking about karate chopping
bitches, I heard Mrs. Jenner knock on the kitchen
door as she let herself in. I was not going to
risk being distracted with listening to her crap.
Moaning about the Tweeds and how kids these
days get away with murder. Trust me love, if it was
that easy to get away with murder, just saying.
Anyways I fucked off to bed, and left Daniel in
her company. I must have been tired because my
head didn't even get chance to sing before it was
morning, and I survived.

Like the robot I became, I got up, went downstairs
and parked my butt on my chair, ready to start my
day. My morning was pretty peaceful after a good
night's sleep. I sat wondering if the smudge on the
window had changed shape. Oh, the excitement.
I was almost certain the smudge was off Daniels

sweaty forehead, from not knowing how close the window was to his face. Or from excitement when fucking Janet pulls up in her car. After his long morning in bed, Daniel finally came downstairs. Sloth like with puffy eyes he made his way into the living room to ask me if I would like a coffee. At this moment the normal and well me, would tell him to sit down, after looking like he has had a rough night then make the coffee myself. But no, instead Mr. paranoia woke up and out of nowhere I instantly concluded that poison was his plan. I really must be such a burden on him. The poor guy looked exhausted! Well planning murder is enough to keep even the strongest of people awake. Why could I not just shake off this illness that had taken over my head? Why did it have to be my head? I wanted to love him so much, my heart hurt from missing him but my head was a different person. My head was broken, cracked all over with every vile thought or feeling leaking out and being carried around my body via bloodstream, like a drug. Even the window smudge was becoming a stranger. So many people around me, yet I am so lonely. Maybe it was the good night sleep or Daniels's poison, either way today I felt different. My head was paranoid, my heart was sad and crying, my blood was boiling with anger, but yet, my body seemed dead and lifeless. I tried so hard to go back to concentrating on the sweaty head print on my window but failed. Instead, I decided to work out what

Daniels's poison was.

After rummaging through my pockets trying to find any clue to what Daniels's poison could be, all I could do was eliminate. Well, I was not allergic to anything that I know of, so an allergic reaction is off the table. Salt? An overdose on salt? Nar, I am pretty sure I could taste that coming plus any pills or medicines. If I was in a moveable state I could do my research, but then could I? I mean if Daniel was stupid enough to poison himself by mistake instead of me then nothing points the finger more than a crazy wife researching poison.

I know my mind is not working right and no sane person would ever assume her husband was trying to kill her without him acting more oddly than Daniel has been. I mean I had no physical evidence. All I have to go off is a conversation my head narrated while watching Daniel and Janet talk. It was all made up really, so why did I believe it so much? What if it is not made up? And my subconscious knew the truth! I did start to feel a little better knowing it could have been my head that had made the whole thing up, but now I was not too sure. The shadow was looming over my head again. I kept trying to reassure myself that it was all in my head, but the counter argument was very convincing. What if I did manage to convince myself that it was all in my head and it was not! What then? I would be a sitting duck. I would not see it coming. Maybe that is a good thing? Leave them to do my dirty work. The debate between me and my head was well on the way.

CHAPTER 7.
BEGINNING OR THE END?

As time became redundant all I could concentrate on was making it through whatever Daniel and Janet were planning. It was certainly an iffy situation I found myself in, as I know fine well Daniel would never hurt me but yet my head didn't want to believe it. Maybe he was poisoning me slowly and that is why I felt so broken inside? That did sound plausible and could have been believed if I was not as liable for my own actions. Not having a single clue of how much time has passed me by today, I continued weighing up every option I had in relation to saving myself.

Stuck in deep thought I noticed condensation filling up my widows as the air became dangerously thin. These are the early warning signs that something big is creeping around the house. Breathing in all my oxygen and turning it to fire! As the dragon prowled around the side of my house, I had no choice but to brace for impact. Before the smell of dragon's breath made its way to my house, I hear the dreaded tap on the back door. Mrs. Jenner was the only one that knocked on the back door. I think she used it in order to ensure entry. Either me or Daniel were in the kitchen, plus the girls played out the back so there was no way to hide or pretend we were out. I am just thankful she had the courtesy to knock before she just walked into my house. I am sure she lived by the same rules as a vampire, once invited in, always invited in! I did put a piece of garlic on my table once while she was around to see what would happen, she didn't fizzle, sizzle or get burnt, in fact she actually picked it up said oh how kind, thank you and put it in her bag. Daniel had found it hilarious.

Garlic aside, with every knock and creek of the door comes with an ear piercing, "Yoo-hoo." She was like a jack in the box. No matter how much you tried to brace yourself for it, it always managed to pop a few blood vessels in your brain. She then popped her head into my living room, greeting me. This was not what I needed right now! Where the fuck was Daniel.

Then out of nowhere I was overcome with the mighty strength to shout, "Daniel." As I had not spoken in so long, in a panic Daniel ran down the stairs just to be welcomed by Mrs. Jenner. Maybe I was getting better? I did speak after all! Well, I said a word at least. Maybe my cracks are healing? It must be a good sign.

Unlucky for Daniel he had just put the kettle on

before running off to the toilet so he had no choice but to offer Mrs. Jenner a drink. Well, she was in and sat comfy, chatting away like a bird staring at a cat through the window. I tried not to listen to her waffle but sometimes it was hard not to, and the way things have been lately, her waffle sounded better than listening to my head. "Me and the neighbours are wondering, how Sammy is?" Let's just be clear. Number one: no one else gave a shit. Number two: she was just being a nosey cow and felt like she was missing out on something. There is no number three, just a two-point attack.

As I sat listening, I heard the chairs squeak along the kitchen floor signalling she must be leaving. Thank God! It was becoming unbearable trying to concentrate on my head talking as well as her. As I heard Daniel enter the living room, without hearing the back door open or close first, I prepared myself for contact. In came Daniel, followed by Mrs. Jenner. What the fucking shit was he doing. He then went on to introduce her as if she was a stranger to me. I am not fucking stupid. My brain is still alive! I am still alive! I was so offended!

"Sam, Mrs. Jenner, who lives next door, has come to visit you. She has been worried with not seeing you out for a while." Err I know who the fuck and where the fuck Mrs. Jenner is and lives. Daniel offered Mrs. Jenner a seat then said, "I will put the kettle on, shall I?" The fucking bastard! I couldn't be the only person that thought all Daniel did was make coffee. Well, I sat there just staring at Mrs. Jenner's mouth move. All I could hear was noise. With her talking, my head talking, the kettle boiling, dogs barking, cars driving.

I really need everything to just shut the fuck up. The colour drained from Mrs. Jenner's face as I turned around to see Daniel white with shock. I was as confused as them. Did that come out my mouth? I was not at all sure but looking at their faces suggest maybe it was a verbal thought. At least Mrs. Jenner has shut up and honestly, I did not feel as angry. Maybe I had reached boiling point and needed to let out some steam. Whatever had happened must have worn out my head as before I realised Mrs. Jenner was gone and Daniel was in the kitchen making food. Poisoned food I bet.

Daniel shouted in from the kitchen, "Sounds like Tweeds have been paid." God knows how or where they get their money from, but I feel some illegal activity is involved. "Hey, I wonder if Mrs. Jenner will call around to fill us in on the gossip?" he said with a little chuckle to himself. Her face was a little funny if I am honest, although I still cannot work out if I am getting better or worse, that is if worse is even possible. Surely starting to say words is a step forward. But after my meeting with Mrs. Jenner, I have doubts. Is this a sign? Am I loosing full control of myself? Or am I just fighting to keep it?

Sitting in my chair I could see puffs of smoke pass my window from a fire the Tweeds had started. I really didn't understand why they needed to start a fire in their garden every time they were out there. All they were doing was drinking and being noisy. I guess it came with the curse of living next door to them. Beer, fire and friends! That is what BFF stands for with that lot. Now and again, I would see their children run up and down past my window. I am not even sure how many children they have now, as I stopped counting at five. I am sure they also have a few grandkids in the mix now though, so God knows how many there are now.

Watching the way those children run around and play it was a wonder they had survived as long as they had. The number of times I heard cars screeching to a holt trying to avoid knocking one of them over was as crazy as my head! And it was always the driver's fault. Never the children's. I know this because after each car screech followed an abusive shout. Either telling a driver to slow down or to learn how to drive. Honestly though, children should not be playing on the road to start with. Maybe I should start to shout for them to slow down your mouth or learn how to parent. That would be a bit rich coming from my mouth, especially with how my parenting skills have been lately.

It did not seem that long before Daniel had brought our food into the living room and placed mine on the coffee table in front of me. He sat with his food on his knee eating while watching the television. We gave up eating our food at the kitchen table a long time ago, although we still made the girls eat there. We had never really been the eat as a family type. The girls were always home and ready for bed before Daniel, so our routines just went with the flow of time. Sitting, listening to Daniel chew his food, while the tele blared and the Tweeds laughed while every beat of their pounding music was like the click of a dial turning up the anger inside me. Even the smell of my food was making me feel angry.

"Please try and eat something Sam."

I had not been able to eat food properly for a while now, in fact I cannot remember the last time I ate anything. While I was in deep though, trying to remember the last time I had eaten food, Daniel repeated himself, but a little louder.

"Sam! Please try and eat something."

Without a word or warning, I slammed my hand down onto the plate of food next to me. Full flat palm splashing food all over the table. Then grabbing anything in its path my hand clasped the biggest hand full of food and slapped it into my mouth. I then turned back to face the window and sat in silence. May not have been much, but at least

I had eaten. Daniel was not impressed. He jumped up, slamming his plate on top of mine before stomping off into the kitchen. It was a good five or ten minutes before he emerged from the kitchen with a dish cloth to clean up my mess. I really wish I could have told him how sorry I was and that it was not my fault. I was losing control of myself.

The guilt was quickly shoved in a pocket allowing me to concentrate on soaking up more anger as if it was the sun. This evening seemed to be going on forever. My head was loud and hurting, the Tweeds were loud, and Daniel was hurting. Today was grating on me like my teeth when I saw Janet. Just thinking of her name makes my blood boil.

As the night continued its never-ending mission to break me, the tension between me and Daniel was getting as loud as the Tweeds. Every two fucking minutes Daniel jumped out of bed to open the window just to slam it shut again a minute later. I don't even think he was warm. He just needed an excuse to bang something to show people he was angry. Whatever his reasons were, it was starting to piss me right off. I just need time to think. I needed some quiet time just to think. Daniel finally gave up on the window bashing and stomped off downstairs. He was not quiet about it either. All I could hear was pots and plates being banged about the kitchen, chairs being slid in and out from under the kitchen table. At least with the window bashing there was a minute of rest between bangs.

My head was not handling today very well at all. Every bang echoed around my head. Every laugh pierced through ears. Everything needed to be quiet! Daniel needed to be quiet! the Tweeds needed to be quiet! My head needed to be quiet! I just needed quiet!

Daniel's bangs became less frequent before he made his way back upstairs and back to bed. "Let's watch tele shall we," he said as he reached for the remote control. I wonder if he knew that by turning on that tele he was turning up the heat to my blood supply. Adding to the noise I already couldn't manage. The night seemed to have settled down to a steady pace. Daniel was much calmer, and the Tweeds seemed to be mellowing.

Before the night was over there was an almighty bang followed by a cheer of celebration. The Tweeds must have put something in their fire and sat, waiting for the outcome. Daniel jumped up and out of bed running to the window. Have you ever had something, or someone make you jump? And the adrenalin shoots straight to your heart causing it to beat like a drum ready to burst its skin? Your head is then torn between fight or flight while your body is stuck between freeze or run. I assumed that was the normal response for any person who had been shocked with an unknown. I had that feeling many times, it never lasts long and it was amazing how much you could feel or think in just a few milliseconds. This time was different for me though. My head or body did not give me a choice. The anger that shot through my body was like nothing else. The shock my system felt was strong enough to have sent me into cardiac arrest. I went straight into fight mode. No thinking, no feeling, just pure fight. I ran down my stairs and straight out the front door as if it was not there. As I stood in my bed clothes, bare foot in my front garden, I just screamed. I screamed so loud, Daniel ran out the house after me. The whole street was outside, staring, gaping at the crazy woman!

For a split second I was able to stop. I was able to think. Looking around, scouting my surrounding like a homing device finding its target. What was I doing! What the actual fuck was I doing. I was starting to panic, with the uncontrollable shaking starting to fog up my head once again. Am I sad? Scared? Angry? I didn't know anymore. There was no pocket labelled unknown. We were not taught about this feeling. How could I manage something that even I don't know? This feeling that lies in the centre of my body so desperate to be freed. But how? How could I possibly know what to do!

"Come on Sam." Daniel took my hand to lead me back inside. The unknown feeling lurking inside my chest gave me no choice but to switch off. Morning came too quick.

CHAPTER 8.
MEET DOCTOR KHAN.

The morning after my melt down came far too quickly. I still had that weird, unknown feeling niggling away inside my chest. As I lay there not knowing what to feel I realised Daniel was not in bed. Weird. I got up to go for a pee. As I sat waiting to finish my morning pee, I could hear Daniel talking in the living room. My first thought was for god's sake, I really cannot be arsed with Mrs. Jenner today. Then I heard a man's voice replying to Daniel. Who the fuck was it? I was not going to find out who it was sat on the loo. Unless it was some weird pervert who likes to watch ladies pee. Well, no one was watching me pee, so I squeezed out the last bit, wiped my bits, washed my hands then proceeded to creep down the stairs. They must have known I was on my way as they stopped talking. Why was I feeling so scared? It was my house, my home, I was the boss around here. As I walked into the living room, I saw Daniel sat on his chair with another guy in mine.

"Sam, this is Doctor Khan."

The guy turned to look at me and stood up to say hello. "Hi Sam, I'm doctor Khan, Daniel has been telling me that you are not feeling very well."

Did he now? I bet he didn't tell you he was planning my murder. Did he? I never said that but thought about it. I just stood there instead, staring at him with a confused face. He was a short fella with a slim build, dark hair and possibly from an Asian background. He did seem nice and well mannered. As he sat back down in my chair he continued to talk to me.

"Sam is it ok if I ask you a few questions?" Daniel looked at me, smiled and nodded his head. I think he knew I was not going to answer myself.

"Now, Sam some of these questions sound strange but I have to ask them, ok?" Again, Dainel nodded his head while looking at me so the doctor could continue.

"Do you think you will, or have you ever had thoughts of harming yourself?" I was too busy trying to get my thoughts in order so by the time I had thought of something to say the moment had passed and Daniel was already answering Dr. Khan's question. In his defence I did not show any indication of answering the doctor but is that justification for him to assume he knows how I feel?

He told him, "No, I don't think so." No! He did not think so?

Daniel and the doctor chatted amongst themselves for a while, with an occasional isn't that right Sam thrown in there. If I am being honest now, all I could think about was why is he was sitting in my chair. I was standing here in the doorway of my living room like a fucking muppet while they both sat there, chatting and smiling. I had enough by this point, so I decided to go and sit in my garden.

As I got to my back door I was hit with a wall of fear, and I just froze. I kept telling myself to just go out. What the fuck was my problem. Just go out. The door is open, all I had to do was put one foot in front of the other and walk. I am not scared of the outdoors so why am I so panicky? If that idiot was not sitting in my chair, I would not be going through this now. I am just praying at this moment that Mrs. Jenner has more sense than gossip because God knows what I would do if her head was to pop around the corner. Luckily, she did. Have more sense that is.

I finally heard the doctor shout into the kitchen, "Bye Sam, I hope we can meet again soon!" I never answered him, nor did I hope we would meet again any time. At least his arse was no longer taking up my space. As I retreated from the war with the outside world and made my way back to my comfort place, Daniel had seen the doctor out and was back in the living room. It may have just been me but the air in the room felt as awkward as having a shit in public.

I was sitting back in my contaminated chair while Daniel wandered around the house like a lost puppy. He eventually came in with a glass of water and two pills placing them on the table next to me before sitting down in his chair. We sat in silence for a minute or two until Daniel built up the courage to ask me to take the pills. I think he was still nervous after the incident with the food.

"Doctor Khan says these pills may help you feel better."

I could hear the concern in his voice, but who was he concerned for? Me? Himself? The girls? The girls were not here so it couldn't be them. Where are my girls? I feel I have not seen them for ages. Without another thought I asked Daniel where my girls were.

"Where are the girls, Daniel?"

"At my mum's love. My mum is going to take care of them until you feel better. Please take your pills."

Oh, I will take my pills alright. I threw the pills to the back of my throat, swigged a little water before stomping off to my bed, badass style.

Jokes aside I had never felt so lonely than I did in that very moment. What if they forgot me? Or I never got better? What If I stopped remembering them? Their faces, their smells? Emily's butter-wouldn't-melt smile standing next to Amelia's cheeky little face. Is this it? Have I lost the battle against myself? Maybe I should just give in and let Daniel put me out of our miseries. I had given up. I had nothing left to live for. My life had not been my own for a while, my own children don't even feel my own. What was the point?

For days I lay in my bed, only waking to take the pills Daniel insisted on feeding me. I didn't even care if they were poison, in fact I hoped they were. I hated the person I had become that much, suicide seemed a luxury I was not allowing myself to have. I needed to suffer. Through my eyes life was the biggest punishment I could endure.

Allowing the days to pass me by I started to feel a little more in control. As I started to fall back into my old routine of getting up, going downstairs, sitting in my chair, I became more and more awake each day. I started to feel ok. I had even managed to sit in my back garden on some days. Maybe there was hope for me after all.

The time had finally come for my girls to come back home. Awe their beautiful faces, I love them so much. Running around, giggling, I even missed their bickering. I was starting to become me again.

How lucky was I? I could have easily thrown myself off a bridge or in front of a bus, but compassion for others saved me. What happens when compassion is lost? And we can only feel that if we rid the world of our existence, maybe it could be a better place for our loved ones. What about the other poor people, trapped in their own minds fighting? I had Daniel at least. Despite me being "poorly" (that's what I am going to call it now) he stood by me. He looked after me. Without him would I have ever got better? I had my kids to fight myself for. Not everyone had something to fight for.

Remembering Ralph, yeah, he had a family of support but he still lost his fight. And his poor mum and sister were left to live the rest of their days out in grief, maybe even guilt that they could not save him. Who was the selfish one in all that? Ralph for wanting to end his suffering? Or his family for encouraging him to suffer more to save their own feelings? Not everyone is strong enough to get better. Some people don't even want to get better. Life was short when your happy or content, but believe me, when you are not happy or suffering, a lifetime is not short enough.

My life was slowly getting back on track, don't get me wrong I was not fixed, but I was lucky. I don't think any person can fully recoup, not when mental health is involved. You can only learn to adapt. Conceal, don't feel, move on. I say that to myself a lot. I heard that in a movie once and it means more than some people can grasp. I know people say don't bottle it all up or why don't you talk about it? And for some people that works, not everyone is the same. We were not all manufactured in a warehouse with machines ensuring we are all wired the same. No we are all made with our very own unique genes.

Our minds are a valuable asset to life. Behind everyone and everything there is a mind, whether it is thinking or not is another question. Everything that has been built, made, born and created has started from a mind, not always a good mind but nevertheless a mind. We should take more care of them, learn how to help the people at war with their own minds to take care of them. I was lucky so far.

CHAPTER 9.
STILL IN THE SHADOWS.

A year on from my downfall and I had managed to live to spend another Christmas with my little family. I was given the chance to celebrate them turning another year older, celebrate another year of being Daniels's wife, another year of being a mum. But also, another year of silent suffering. It had been hard but like any great actor would, I played the part with a smile. Living in fear that one day I may lose the ability to keep the control I had just got back. With no choice I soldiered on.

Although my days were becoming brighter, there still hung a shadow of darkness over my head. People still looked at me funny, the parents at school still whispered amongst themselves, people still spoke to me with caution. I remember one day as I was picking up the girls from school, and one of the parents barged past me muttering, "Like mother, like daughter." As I turned around to face her, she gave me the most disgusted look. What the fuck was her problem. As I made my way to the door where Emily was let out and her teacher called me inside.

"Emily has hit a boy in our class, we would be grateful if you can ask dad to have a word with her as this behaviour is not tolerated at our school!" Woah! Hold on. My child does not hit other children for nothing, and I am her mother! I am perfectly capable of talking to her myself! Yeah, I never actually said that. But I strongly thought it. Who the fuck was she to play me down in front of my child. And while I was on the path of mad thinking, why the fuck did that kids mum feel she could barge past me muttering shit! Emily stomped out of the school doors and bolted straight for the car. I left her to have some space while I went to get Amelia.

The drive home was unusually quiet. Emily was just sitting, silently staring out of the car window. Amelia knew something was wrong as she just sat humming tunes to herself quieter than normal, in her own happy little world. During the silence I could not help but wonder if I had cursed Emily with a head like mine. She had always seemed happy. Or had I always been to preoccupied to take note. This kind of damage couldn't be undone. Just made easier to accept. As we pulled up on the drive Amelia could not wait to get out of the car and run inside, Emily was more sloth like, no emergency there. This time is as good as time as any to have a word with her.

"Emmy? Do you want to tell me what happened in school today?"

The second them words left my mouth her reply came as quick as Monday morning. "It's all your fault! Why do you have to be my mum! I hate you!" As the door slammed behind her all I could do was stand and think. Wow! As I slowly slid down to the floor, my head started to tick over like a car refusing to start. Does she really hate me? Am I really that bad? I know I have had my moments, but I have tried my best. They know that, right? Maybe they don't know. How could they. They cannot feel what I feel, just like they cannot think what I think. Is it time to ask for an outside view of myself? I mean its only risking my self-portrait, people have already seen what they have seen. I have no idea how long I sat on my driveway thinking before Daniel pulled up in his car. He seemed to have one of his cannot be arsed with this shit faces on him.

"Come on love, let's go inside," he said as he walked straight past me and into the house. Nice, even he hates me today. I sat there for a minute longer before I went inside. I did notice though that I had started to get that weird, unknown feeling in my chest again. It really was a weird feeling, a bit like a nervous twinge in my heart that was pumping out every other kind of feeling.

Once I got inside Daniel was already upstairs with the girls. I could hear them giggling so not everything was bad. I bet he thinks he is fucking superman now. All I was able to do at this moment was keep remembering to interrupt my thoughts. Remember Sam, conceal it, feel nothing. Move the fuck on. Make tea like a good little mummy. Well, I was definitely not in the mood to make tea but did it anyways. As I scouted around my kitchen trying to decide what I could be arsed making, Daniel decided to show his face.

"Sam, I've spoken with Emily."

"Noodles, they can have noodles." Then I grabbed the noodle packets to start cooking. I was not in any kind of mood to talk any more than I wanted to cook. I just tried to pretend everything was ok and that this would pass. I was just not expecting it to pass like a bad fart.

Once the girls had eaten, super dad Daniel took them upstairs to get them settled ready for bed. Emily had barely looked at me this evening with not a single word spoken. My heart was slowly breaking, and a broken heart is something I have never really had to deal with. I have learnt the hard way what happens when the cracks in my mind start to show, but my heart. That was something I have never felt I needed to worry about. Will I lose my compassion through the cracks? What about love? Will all that drain away like water in a holy bucket? Love and compassion saved me last time, maybe my luck is running out. It has to some time, I guess.

Once the girls had settled, Daniel was ready to

try and talk, again. This time though I had no distractions or excuses. I did try to ignore him, but he would just not shut up. So, I asked him what happened with Emily at school. Daniel told me that some of the children at school had made up a scary story. A story of psycho Sam! She lurked in puddles waiting and watching children play and if you walk near a puddle psycho Sam would grab your ankle and pull you into the puddle, never to be seen again. Apparently, it happened to a boy once. Daniel went on to say that a boy pushed Emily over into a puddle told her to go see her mum, then everyone laughed at her. Emily then got up and punched the boy in the face, before being taken inside.

I needed a few minutes to think this over. My head was not processing information very well and I could tell Daniel was losing patience.

He shouted, "You cannot just ignore this, Sam!"

I was not trying to ignore him or the issue, I was just trying to get my thoughts in order. My head felt like a bag of scrabble pieces that were being shaken, I just needed to get a little order.

Daniel stood up with frustration and calmly said, "I cannot do this again." He then walked off into the kitchen.

"Do what exactly?" I said abruptly while following him in the kitchen.

Daniel snapped back pretty quickly with, "This!

You! Your head! Can you not see what you are doing to us!"

He spoke as if I was to blame. As if I was in control of manipulating my own mind. It was not my fault and him of all people should be able to understand that! Daniel's speech was far from over, in fact he carried on shouting for a good while. I am surprised he did not give himself a hernia the way he was going on.

"All you do is sit there, saying nothing! Doing nothing! Do you even love me? What about the girls? Do you even care?"

So many questions I barely had time to answer him. By the time I had managed to think of an answer he had moved on to ask another. My head was not built for such bombardment. Eventually I heard the girls starting to cry so I stood up ready to go to their aid when Daniel stopped me in my tracks.

"Sit back down! You have done enough damage for one day!" He then turned around and headed up the stairs to the girls. Super dad to the recuse again.

What was I supposed to do? I couldn't change who I had become and trust me I had tried. Am I facing losing my family again? I really do not know what I am supposed to do, never mind how to fix things.

Emily was right, it was my fault. I was psycho Sam.

So seen as I was being treated as some

misunderstood villain, it was time to up my game. I need to hatch a cunning plan to regain my former glory and unmask the real villain in all this. Janet. So, I decided my best form of action would be to confront Mrs. Brocket and fix this.

Mrs. Brocket was the head teacher at the girl's school. With her dirty blond hair and know-it all mannerism, she never had been my number one fan. But that was my plan. Win over the evil headteacher. I have no idea what or how this was going to help but my head was not thinking rationally. This plan was never built to be bullet proof, in fact very little thought at all went into it. All I knew was that the plan could end one of three ways.

Ending one, I win. I rise to victory winning back the love and respect of my family while unmasking the real villain: fucking Janet.

Ending two, Brocket wins! And the super villain AKA me is finally behind bars.

Ending three. And the most probable ending of all. Nothing changes. Well apart from Mrs. Brocket gaining a little extra paperwork and me sounding more of a prick than before I started. Daniel would get to keep his super-dad rank while fucking Janet took over my world.

So, after a full night of thinking how great I would be after I had been into school and fixed everything it was morning. I was running on the power of being over tired, not a great start to anyone's day but a start none the less.

CHAPTER 10.
THE SCHOOL MEETING.

As I started my day with a fresh over tired smile it would not be long until I figure out that reaching this point in my sleepless journey is the worst. You know you need to sleep but you feel there is no hope of it ever happening. Your brain starts to work overtime when at the same time not functioning at all. It is a very strange set up. I am unsure why but once I have broken the tape at the 'over tired' finish line, I am left with a runner's high. I get so much energy I feel I could take on the world.

While some people will experience that burst of energy that you get after passing the tired finish line, some may not have had the chance to such luxury. Running on this kind of power source is absolutely bollocks! It is not just unhealthy, it is unstable, cruel to our minds and sounds no different from taking an illegal drug. You run around all wide eyed not having an ounce of care then all of a sudden, crash! Suddenly you hit the ground. One thing though, being over tired is not addictive.

So, not only was I now running dangerously low on the mental ability to control my own actions, but I was also physically suffering the effects of sleep deprivation. Not a great combo for any super villain getting ready to take back what it truly theirs. But nevertheless I would do what must be done. I hoped. Fingers crossed.

Finally, I started to hear Daniel and the girls getting up ready for their day. I could hear their footsteps moving from one side of their rooms to the next. Isn't it funny that as a mum you get to know exactly who is moving around just by the sound of the footsteps. You can even predict what is going to happen next. For example, Amelia's footsteps move more quickly and lighter than Emily's. Emily has a proper stomp. And right now, I just heard Amelia's quick moving feet run to the bathroom and slam the door which only means one thing! Boom! Boom! Boom! "Hurry up! I need the bathroom!" Emily has never been a morning person and made sure everyone heard it, every day.

It seemed like a lifetime before they were all downstairs. I mean I was running on a hundred minutes per second. And to their amazement, mum had their lunches ready and also a coffee for Daniel.

I would like to say my enthusiasm was shared amongst the tribe, but it was not. I think they were more concerned than anything. Well, Daniel definitely was. His demeanour was more tired and couldn't be arsed today. But that was his problem not mine. I was eager to go by this point! I had the pre-race adrenaline running through my body.

As I was waiting for the girls to finish getting ready, I could not help but stop for a second or two and just stare at them. The feeling I got was like I had met them again for the first time. Emily was all sighs and tuts, but Amelia was the opposite. She was so happy, humming tunes to herself while putting on her socks. I could not help but get overwhelmed with pride. Even Emily's grumpy face made me smile.

Getting into the car was no different than any other morning. Emily stomped out to the car opening the door as forcefully as possible before slamming her backside down on the seat. She then waited, with her arms folded for me to close the car door. Amelia, well, she was just Amelia. So happy, skipping to the car without a care in the world. I really wish I could join her in that little world she lives in. I imagine it being so happy and peaceful, with sunshine bursting through the cloud, miles of bright green grass covered in a carpet of flowers and little bumble bees humming sweet little tunes. I couldn't help but hope she lives in her own world forever.

While driving to school I thought I would take a page out of Amelia's book and try and create my own imaginary world. I started with a bright blue sky and fresh green grass with the odd daisy dotted around. It really was a peaceful place to be.

What would have normally been a super stressful journey had turned out ok, thanks to Amelia's world. Anyone that had to do the school run understands how shit it is. All it consists of is traffic and rude parents. Driving past a high school is worse. That is a different kind of traffic. Millions of teenage children with no regards for safety pushing each other, walking in the road like they own it. It's the teachers that have to stand on each corner I feel sorry for. Telling people they cannot park there, trying to keep the children in order while trying not to cry. I would not be able to do that job.

Seeing as I was in my Amelia world, pulling up to school was no bother at all. Emily jumped out the car before I even had the chance to fully pull up the handbrake. Running so fast into school like a hoard of zombies were chasing her. I had a feeling though it was due to the fact somebody might see her with "psycho Sam" and not because she was excited to go to school. I was fine with this though because I was going to fix things and make them better. After Amelia skipped off happily to her class, I was then on the path to the school office to tackle Mrs. Brocket.

As I waited in the school office for the receptionist to get off the phone, I started to lose my newfound energy. What the actual fuck am I planning on saying? I know I came here to defend Emily but how? Shit!

Finally, the receptionist finished on the phone, open her little window and asked, "How can I help?" I strongly felt the urge to tell her I was beyond help but I just said I was Emily Nichols mum and wanted to speak with the headteacher. Oh, and I said please. In that moment I prayed so hard she would not ask what it was regarding. Which she did and for fucks sake I did not think this far ahead. I really had missed out the middleman on this plan. The plan only consisted of going to school, speaking to Mrs. Brocket then everything would be fixed. Magic!

I ended up pulling a really odd-looking face and said, "Emily! Obviously!" Which she did not seem impressed with because she pulled her face back and told me to take a seat before slamming her stupid little window.

At this point I was feeling more stupid than epic. I know I had a plan but what was I actually going to say to her? What was I wanting to fix? She was not a marriage counsellor no more than she was a psychiatrist. She was a headteacher, of a school. As I waited all I could do was repeat the words "fucking shit" over and over in my head.

After twenty minutes or so of waiting and hearing the words "fucking shit" play on repeat in my head, the receptionist finally made an appearance.

She opened her little window, smiled at me and said, "Sorry, Mrs. Brocket is busy today, and won't be able to see you."

Well! I'd like to say I stood up nice and calm, smiled and said, "Oh! No problem just let me know when she is free." I then left the building, went home and sat down with a nice coffee. Now, I like to think by this point you know enough about me to understand that did not or would not happen. Instead, I stood up, shouted, "Are you fucking kidding me." Then I charged to the office window like I was on fire.

Don't worry she closed that stupid little window before I had the chance to swan dive through it. All she did before sitting back in her chair was shrug her shoulders while mouthing the word, "Sorry," like it was not her fault. It may not have been her fault but at this point I wanted to speak to Mrs. Brocket.

I continued to stomp and shout, demanding to see Mrs. Brocket through the little window for a good ten minutes before heading back to my car. I never caught on to the fact that Mrs. Brocket being busy was actually my get out of jail free card. I mean if she had come out, I had no idea what to say, even more so, now I had made a scene.

Sitting in my car feeling like an absolute dick, I decided to try and escape back into Amelia's world, only this time it was not as bright. The grass had turned a dirty brown colour while the clouds were darkened grey with a chance of rain. This morning was about making things better for Emily, not darkening Amelia's world too. I mean what exactly was I trying to achieve? Well, if it was to dig down another few inches in my own grave then welldone Sam, give yourself a clap.

Honestly though, why did I not just keep my cool? Is it that hard for me to just shut my mouth or just say ok and leave?. Before I even realised what was happening, I was already in the middle of kicking off. Fuck's sake, I really did not see any way this could be fixed. If I had just calmly explained my reasons for being there, maybe they could or would have been more understanding. Instead, I have just proven the concerns they already had.

By this point I had risen so high with the power of being over tired that I was in mid-air ready to crash land. How dark must my life become that I can not even imagine being in a better place. Is there even a guiding light at the end of my tunnel? Maybe I was the cat in the rat race chasing fucking Janet, who had my light. Oh, she made me so mad, that woman!

Eventually I made my way home. I have no idea how. I don't even remember getting through my front door. I wonder if I even stopped at traffic lights. It is a strange feeling being in a place, then realising you have no clue how you even got there. It is a bit like when you go to the same place every day, say maybe work or school and one day on your way to the shops you end up parked outside either school or work. You then think "shit" and have to turn your car around. I cannot be the only person that has done that.

As it turned out while I was unknowingly making my way home, Daniel had received a phone call from Mrs. Brocket. At least I know now why she was too busy to talk to me. Because she was talking to fucking super dad over there. Why could she have not just spoken to me while I was there? I could have explained things. Daniel didn't know shit and it was me that had asked to speak to her. I was Emily's parent too. Do I not have a say anymore? Is anyone on my side? What even is the point to my existence? The phone call was not in my favour and did me no favours at all.

The next few days were very quiet and awkward. Although I was trying my best to carry on, Daniel still did not seem to want to trust me. I felt I was relieved from all my duties as a mother and wife. Plus, stupid fucking Janet was back, picking up and bringing my girls back from school. Day by day the control over my own head was becoming less, all I needed was patience. If you should never kick a man when he is down, then how come the second I slipped, people made sure I hit the ground? Maybe me getting better put a spanner in Janet's plan to get rid of me. Maybe Daniel did not want me to get better either and only in death do

we part. Why could he not have just carried on.
Instead of kicking me down, why not just look
past it like always and let me catch my breath.
Instead, he had shown me that no matter how
much I try my best, it will never be good enough.
I am branded by mental health and fear I always
will be.

CHAPTER 11.
ROUND TWO.

As round two of the break downs was upon me life around me was changing. This was not my doing but the doing of others. Others getting ready for me to go off the rails again. Putting up their defences before it was too late. Following their own policies and procedures to ensure their own safety. I would have been fine if people around me would have let me be fine, but instead they banished me to a life of crazy. Every time they got jittery, I got side benched. I would not mind but I only had one outburst that was public and the rest were in my head. I was left feeling outcast and alone. This time I knew what to expect, but so did everyone else. I was ready to fight myself whilst everyone else was already running. Last time I survived with Daniel's love and support. This time I felt, he had opened the door ready for me to fall in, so what was the point in fighting anymore. People were expecting me to break, I never was a people pleaser, so I hung on for as long as I had control.

I still was managing to leave the house, although

Daniel AKA super dad still thought it would be best that Janet did the school run. Fucking Janet! I really did have hate for that woman.

With every walk or shopping trip I took, it added more and more troubles to my life pockets, my outdoor activities became less frequent. Every time a person laughed, I assumed they were laughing at me. When I saw two people having a conversation, again I assumed they were talking about me. This went on for a few weeks. With each passing week a different life pocket being filled. One week could be paranoia and the next anger or even sadness. It was a hard pill to swallow seeing people have friends when you know you never will. I even found myself hating children just for being happy with their mums, life did not seem fair to me.

As my pockets were starting to weigh me down, shopping became hard work. Trying to concentrate on not being a weirdo or drawing attention to myself was becoming very challenging indeed. I remember the last time I went to the supermarket, and by the sounds of things so did everyone else. It was not entirely my fault and if I am honest, it was not as bad as people made it out to be.

This day I went to the supermarket to buy a few bits, like milk and bread, the basics. Now, on top of people not keeping their distance from me and that stupid music they play in supermarkets, a child insisted on squeaking his shoes on the floor around the fucking shop. I managed to finish my shop and make it safely to the checkout just to find that the squeaky kid and his mum were in the queue behind me. Now our own personal space is something we are entitled to even in a supermarket. As the cashier was scanning my groceries, I was just throwing them into my trolley while behind me the squeaky kids mum had no sense of space as she kept bumping me with her trolley. All this time that damn kid and his shoes had been squeaking. I nearly made it but as I was about to pay, her trolley bumped into me causing me to drop my purse. Without even the slightest of thought I pushed her trolley back into her knocking her backwards onto her arse then turned to the kid and told him if he didn't stop squeaking them fucking shoes, I would take them off him. All I could say is thank goodness for contactless, I just swiped my card and left.

The incident did not end there, as I have mentioned earlier. I am no way able to leave anyplace gracefully while angry or embarrassed. So, as I left the supermarket in a hurry all I could think about was getting to my car, then home. With no time to spare and a security guard on my tail, the last thing I was looking at was the height of the curb in which my trolley needed to get up. Have you ever rammed a shopping trolley into a high curb? It is not recommended. I hit the curb so hard the back end of the trolley lifted up with me still holding on to it. My shopping dropped everywhere along with any pride I had left. I also broke my wrist. After getting home from my trip to A&E that was rudely followed by a visit from the police, I decided not to go shopping at that supermarket again, plus I was barred for assaulting customers. But again, it was not entirely my fault.

It was only around a week later that my little walks around the block stopped. And I know I have said this before, but this incident was not fully my fault either. Over the years I have become accustomed to the Tweeds and their antics. They are even tolerable on some levels. Although my tolerance levels seem to vary, this evening my minimum level was the highest so there was no room for error. As always, I set off from my house slowly, strolling around the street in a big circle until I was back home. I heard somewhere that fresh air did you good. I tried to not make a habit of leaving my house when the Tweeds were out after my last meltdown but this day, I needed the walk. I left the house already pissed off with Daniel and thought the walk may help clear my head. I may have mentioned something earlier in the evening about Janet being a bitch that upset Daniel as he thought I should be more grateful for her help. Then I may have said something along the lines of, "I would be grateful if she fucked off and took you with her!" Cutting a long story short, I was pissed off, Daniel was pissed off, so I went for a walk.

As I left my house slamming the door behind me, one of the Tweeds made a comment about someone being on one again. It sounded more like, "Uh oh! looks like someone is on one again!" And more of a cheer than a comment. Determined not to let them push me over, I went about my walk. My head was getting so loud I was unable to concentrate on my own thoughts. Why did I hate Janet so much? And why the fuck did Daniel keep defending her? My hate for her could not be her fault. I didn't even remember why I hated her, all I knew was that the hate ran deep no matter what my reasons where. As for Daniel, maybe he is right, I needed to be more grateful. Although in my defence it was hard to be grateful when someone was so perfect, and so happy that your own kids would rather spend time with her than you. Also, should I be grateful that my own husband looks happier talking to her than me. Fucking Janet. I remembered why I hated her now. Maybe it was her fault, she knew full well what she was doing.

By the time I was back near my house, I was angrier than I had originally been when I set out. I found myself walking faster just to get home quicker. The Tweeds were still outside and by the looks of the freshly lit fire, they were not planning on going inside anytime soon either. I was unable to concentrate on my thoughts, all I could hear was their laughter. Laughter clouding up my head as if it was the smoke from the fire. By the time I had reached my gate I was so enraged no one was safe. Without any warning I walked up my garden path to pick up an old bucket we keep outside. We left it there to catch rain so we could water our garden guilt free in a drought. I will add that my wrist was still broken, so it was a one hand job. I then took the bucket poured it over the Tweed's fire and told them to, "Fuck off inside."

Mrs. Tweed was not happy. She got up from her lawn chair screaming, "Who the fuck do you think you are!" She then swung her arm and smacked the bucket right out my hand. Now this next bit is not my proudest moment, although she had it coming. Before the bucket hit the floor, I had given her such a whack in the face with my cast she was fighting to stay on her feet. Daniel had rushed out by this point as Mr. Tweed pointed over to him insisting, he come over and puts a leash on his dog. Daniel quickly grabbed my arm to drag me inside, he never was one to stand and fight. As I got to my front door I saw Mrs. Jenner from the corner of my eye, standing there not even trying to hide the fact she was a nosey cow. I managed to tell her to get the fuck inside as well before Daniel threw me through the front door.

Although this time did not end with a visit to A&E,

not for me anyways, it did end with a visit from the police. After Daniel had explained my issues, they agreed not to arrest me on the condition I revisit the doctor. Daniel assured them that he would call the doctor first thing to arrange an appointment for me. As soon as the police left, Daniel made his way upstairs to bed without saying a single word. I knew he needed some space, so I just made myself comfy on my chair and waited for morning. At least the Tweeds had shut up!

The rest of the night was a blur, it was as if I had been drifting in and out of consciousness. I felt like I had been awake all night but asleep at the same time. I don't recall having any dreams or even thinking for that matter, I think I had just switched off.

As promised, the next day Daniel called the doctor's office and was able to speak with Dr. Khan. I was not in any way able to take in anything he was saying. All I remembered was staring at Daniel's phone in the middle of the coffee table hearing them talk to each other on loudspeaker. Even though I could hear them talking I was not actually able to listen to them. It was as if I had died inside, and nothing was making sense.

Daniel and Dr. Khan had decided it would be best if I did not go out by myself until my head was fully better. I was also put on a waiting list to see a counsellor to help me deal with my thoughts and feelings. Fingers crossed that I was either better or dead by then, so I did not have to go. Talking about my troubles was just not for me.

It was pretty much the day after I smacked the Tweeds that I lost my freedom and once again became confined to my sitting room chair. Well maybe lost was not the right word, more like surrendered my freedom. I didn't put up a fight or even give any thought or care to the matter. I just sat and said nothing.

I became quite the expert in just sitting and saying nothing after that point. I did not even care that Daniel or fucking Janet were getting ready to pounce any day now and take the last piece of life I have left. They could have already done it. I didn't care enough to even notice.

I couldn't even begin to tell you how many days and nights I spent in that chair, just sitting. I didn't even know if I had been eating or drinking. I just didn't know. One thing I did know though was how horrible I had become. Not only to myself but to the people that surround me. Daniel, my girls! Even Mrs. Jenner and the Tweeds. And possibly Janet. They did not need to feel the backlash of my suffering. The suffering was my own, in my own head, in my own body so how was I still able to project my own bad vibes on others?

I felt upset that I was hurting others especially my girls, but I also felt mad. Mad that no one was helping me or understanding me. I felt angry that I was just left here, in this stupid fucking chair by myself. I am not a monster, I am still me.

After reflecting on how nasty I had started to become to the people around me, I began to realise that maybe the person I used to be really was gone and may not come back. You could bounce back from a bad fall, but the fear of it happening again will always be with you. Maybe that was what had happened? I had a bad fall and the fear of me falling again is the cause of me falling again.

CHAPTER 12.
MEET APRIL.

As Daniel became more distant and the girls started to spend more and more time in their rooms, I was left alone to suffer. With only the four walls and my own head as company my life was getting pretty grim. I know I have been like this before but for some reason this time was different. I was more angry, more physical and definitely more vocal. As my own family was starting to resent my company, I started to feel angrier. Angry that I was suffering by no fault of my own. Would I have even got poorly again if there were some understanding of my mental state? I often asked myself "why me?" I won't sit here and say that I would never wish this illness on anyone, because I would be lying. I sometimes wished Daniel could feel how I felt, think how I think, then maybe he would not be as quick to shut me out. To be fair to him though we have gone from very little issues to life changing problems, and I understood he was tired, but so was I.

After a while on the waiting list, I got a visit from

a counsellor. Well at least I think she was one. Her name was April and she came to my house to see me as going out was hard enough without going to a place I did not want to. She seemed like a nice girl. Softly spoken with a compassionate demeaner. Her hair had been dyed a dark red that had a few good washes since her last hair dye, but it fit in with her style. As a whole she gave off a bit of a free spirit vibe which was nice.

April being in my home did not feel as space invading as I thought it would have, in fact it was a bit like having a friend around for the first time. She was not as dismissive as other people had become and seemed interested in searching for my views on the situation without being intrusive. Although I could not bring myself to speak to her, she still managed to connect somehow with me and made me feel more like a person instead of the monster I felt people had become scared of.

It had not been that long before Daniel piped up and started to fill in the blanks. it was interesting to get an insight into his prospective, but I still could not help but become overwhelmed.

As they spoke amongst themselves trying to include me in the conversation, I could not help but wish for them to piss off. I know she was here to help me, and Daniel was trying his best, but I had started to hate everything by this point. Listening to Daniel telling his version of our story, which I will add was a lot different to my version was heart breaking while at the same time quite irritating. Heart breaking as I understood how much he had tried but irritating because he could not see how hard I had also tried or how much pain I had been in. As Daniel continued to tell his story to April, I tried my best to build myself up to speak. I had never really been one to share my feelings but listening to him speak I was beginning to wish I could.

His version of events seemed a lot more peaceful than mine, I suppose that was because he could not hear my head. All he saw was me sitting in silence for weeks. Yeah, I know all I did was sit, but for me it was far from silent. He also pointed out how I showed no emotion or feeling which is somewhat true. I may not have shown feeling but I definitely had felt feelings on a massive scale.

Now and again, April would ask me questions like, "How were you feeling when you were sitting in silence?" Or, "How were you feeling before you hit the lady next-door?" I could not answer her, of course, but I did try and think about how I felt so it was not a complete waste of time. I actually started to feel angry just thinking about hitting lady Tweed. It was as if I had travelled back in time to that exact moment. And if April was trying to ask me if I regretted it? No, I didn't and would do it again, happily.

While my head was preoccupied with the memories I was encouraged to remember, April had said her goodbyes and had left by the time I returned to the present time. The session was not a complete waste of time as Daniel seemed to have perked up a little now, he has got a few things off his chest. I, on the other hand, was left trying to close back up each pocket they had both opened.

It was strange to see how from the outside I seemed silent and uncaring, when on the inside it was louder than a rave riddled with every feeling available. I just assumed that whatever I was feeling on the inside showed on the outside, and that Daniel should have known how I was feeling. Now I know that was not the case and from his point of view I seemed like a heartless bitch that clearly did not care. Did this mean all the times I had felt love or happiness, Daniel did not know it? Were all the times I felt excitement or disappointment for my own benefit? And shared with no one? My outlook on life had changed and I did not take change lightly. Suddenly, each and every life pocket burst open like a firework display.

What else had I gotten wrong? I felt lied to, betrayed by everyone I knew. Had I been so self-absorbed that I was not able to see how I was being perceived? This opened so many more doors for me. I mean what else could I have not known? How blind had I actually been. One thing I did know and that was that my pockets had burst beyond repair. It was a mess, every thought, every feeling all in one place like several jigsaw puzzles mixed together just waiting to be put back in their own boxes. I never was one for jigsaw puzzles.

I had spent the rest of that night on my chair, stewing in my own self-hatred. I have no idea if I slept, but the morning came as quick as the night went. Before too long Daniel was up getting the girls ready for school. I was getting used to everyone moving around me as if I was a piece of furniture. Sad really as I want nothing more than to be the mum I should be. To rub salt in my wounds they did not even know I am crying inside. Crying for one of them to say, "Come on mum," and take hold of my hand. It was not the girl's fault, this was life for them, it was what they were used to. I really wished I could tell them how sorry I was and that I loved them more than I could say.

I began to wish I had jumped off that bridge to save them from a mum like me. Their lives would be so much easier if I was dead. Daniel would be set free from the burden I brought, and the girls wouldn't be bullied as much. I could still do it, nothing was stopping me, and it was always better late than never. As I weighed the pros and cons my death may bring, I concluded that being dead would affect the girls more than staying alive. So I chose to continue to suffer rather than upset the girls even more.

As I sat sorting through the pieces of sadness from within, I saw Daniel run to the window then shout for the girls. The anger inside me boiled up like heartburn. Quicker than a coin flip I went from feeling so sorry for myself to being super angry. Not just angry, but super angry. I hated everything. I hated Daniel, I hated Janet, I even hated the table next to me. I hated the table so much I managed to kick it over and kept kicking it.

Without realising Daniel had come back into the house shouting, "What the fuck is wrong with you?" He must have scared the shit out of me because I just froze. As I stood there trying to catch my breath, it became harder and harder to breathe. It felt as if someone had punched me so hard in my chest my heart had become lodged in my throat. Daniel kept telling me to, "Sit down and try to relax," but the panic overtook my body as I kept pushing him away. I really thought this was it for me, had I actually given myself a heart attack? Was I going to die? I should have been happy that I did not have to kill myself as my body was going to do that for me, but I was not. I was scared shitless. After what felt like a lifetime I eventually started to calm down. All I could do was sit in my chair and try to make sense of things. I eventually found out that I was having a panic attack and not a heart attack.

After that day, things only got worse, my head started to get loud, and my insides were being eaten away by feelings like maggots on a rotting corpse. That strange feeling I had experienced before was back. For the life of me I could not work out what this feeling was, no matter how much I tried. It was as if each bad feeling had emerged together to create one new feeling. Half the time I was not sure if I was angry, sad or nervous, it was very unsettling.

Early Monday morning, I woke up to blue skies and birds chirping. My head was banging and the birds really needed to shut the fuck up. Honestly, I felt like going outside and shaking them out the tree. Don't worry I didn't, even I am not that nasty. The sound of chirping birds was soon drowned out by Daniel and the girls. Amelia could not find her shoe, Emily was just being grumpy and as for Daniel, well he was just Daniel. After the weekend I was not feeling too bad. Daniel had become more withdrawn from me, and the girls kept their distance but other than that nothing was new.

As I saw Janet pull up in her car, I told myself I was fine. Daniel shouted for the girls, I was still fine. The girls ran outside, and Amelia, bless her she is such a loving girl, hugged Janet. I was not fine. That fucking stupid bitch. Oh, I was so mad. I couldn't remember the last time any of my girls hugged me, never mind smiled at me. Then followed Daniel. Smiling as they chatted. He never smiled at me anymore. He was my husband. They were my children. Then Janet touched his shoulder. The shoulder touching was nothing new, and I had seen it happen a million times, but this time was different. I was different.

Overpowered by jealousy I got up off my chair and charged towards the window. Making one massive bang on the window I turned to head out the door. I stormed down the path trampling on anything in my way. All I could remember saying, well screaming is, "I am going to fucking kill you!" As I flew for Janet, Daniel came to her rescue. Standing between us like a stiff beef patty. I just kept pushing and shouting. I could see my girls crying in the car which infused me with more anger. Look what she had done. Then I just started to scream, "You did this! You did this!" Daniel told Janet to just go and looking petrified she got in her car, then started to drive away. Watching her drive away, taking my children, I could not breathe. As she got out of sight I just fell to the floor and cried. And when I say cried it was a snot dribbling cry. Very dignified.

After that morning, the school had decided it was best for the girls to go and stay with Daniel's mum. I also had another visit from Dr. Khan and his sidekick April. I would like to say things started to get better but sadly for me they did not. This time I was properly broken, Daniel was breaking, and my girls were gone. I had been falling for so long that rock bottom had to be close.

CHAPTER 13.
HAVE I LOST?

A week or two had passed since I tried to kill Janet, and my life had become so empty. Daniel was acting like I did not exist, my girls were still gone and once again it was just me and my head. Daniel started to work more as he has had so much time off work to be with me, he had to put in more hours. Or so he said. The street seemed quieter, and Mrs. Jenner stopped visiting. I became so lonely I actually started to miss Mrs. Jenner's company. I even hoped for a Tweed party just to drown out my own thoughts. All I could do was cry. I sat and cried so much. My life was worthless, I felt like no one cared, I was just left to fade away. I was forgotten.

I know from the outside that my actions seemed selfish and were deemed unacceptable, but none of it was intentional. I knew I had always been an unsociable person but I never wanted to be disrespectful or harmful for that matter. I loved my family, I loved Daniel and missed my girls greatly, so why could I not shake my head and become the person I wanted to be. I did not want to be like this or feel like this. I got no pleasure from draining the life out of Daniel or forcing the girls out of their home. I helped to build this home, it was supposed to be full of love, happiness and memories, not resent, sadness and regrets. Why was this so hard to shake off?

As I sat thinking about everyone I had lost or hurt, I started to panic. The panic attack was back, only this time I was alone. Alone and scared. What had I done so wrong to deserve such punishment? I paced up and down my living room with such panic, wondering what I was supposed to do. I had never felt so frightened before. Once the light-headedness set in, I had no choice but to sit down.

My day seemed so long, I could not wait for Daniel to come home just so I was not on my own. I had never really been on my own before, so this was a new experience for me. Maybe it was karma catching up with me for not making more of an effort to play outside with Jessica, or for getting fed up with Mrs. Jenner's spontaneous visits. Either way the shoe was definitely on the other foot.

It was pretty late by the time Daniel got home. He walked through the door said, "HI," then went to get a shower. I did not mind him not speaking to me that much as he was still company at the end of the day, so I did start to feel a little better just knowing he was there. It was not long before Daniel finished his shower and came downstairs to sit in his chair. Only five, maybe ten minutes passed when he stood up and said, "Right, I am going for a walk." He then left. Maybe he has had a bad day? I had never known Daniel to just go out for a walk, well unless he was nipping to the shop or taking the girls out. I just tried not to think too much into it at the time.

An hour had passed before Daniel got back home. That was some walk if I do say so myself. Maybe his pockets were getting full, and they need organising. Walks alone used to help me. As Daniel came in, he plonked himself on his chair then kicked off his trainers. He let out a long sigh before turning on the tele. I asked him if he was ok, but he just nodded his head without even looking away from the tele.

Another hour had passed, and I had definitely had enough. The silence broke with only a little sigh now and again, it was grating on me big time. So I asked him what his fucking problem was. His response was, "Nowt". No scream or shout Just emptily said, "Nowt." That was not even an answer for fuck's sake. Was he trying to give me a taste of my own medicine? Showing me what life on the other side looks like? Maybe he was just genuinely tired? Or maybe, he was secretly meeting up with Janet and they both planned to run off in the sunset together. I bet that's it. Even though the other reasons sounded more plausible, I chose to stick with the Janet theory.

As the night progressed, I tried so very hard to steer my thoughts away from the affair I believed Daniel and Janet were having. The more I sat there thinking, the worse things became. The feelings where becoming real. What was left of my mentality was quickly turning to mush. My head was beginning to make up different scenarios that involved Janet and Daniel, just to replay them, over and over as if they had really happened. I was somehow convincing myself that this shit was really happening. Despite my efforts to steer clear, I was heading straight for a canyon with an out of order sign on my brakes.

I was now officially lost. Lost as well as unsure. I had lost my place in this world, unsure of how real my own existence had been. Every part of my life had changed and with my memories starting to fade the only thing my head or body could feel was betrayal. What was I supposed to do? How was I supposed to tackle this without physical contact? Although, rugby tackling Janet the next time she stepped out of her car could be movie material.

I honestly could not tell you how much of that night I had sat thinking up shit and how much of it I spent dreaming up shit, all I know was the night seemed never ending and whichever way I did it, my head was full of shit. When the morning finally arrived, I was left feeling beaten. Have you ever had a dream that's been so intense, that when you wake in the morning your left feeling unsure if it had actually happened? The feeling so strong it sticks with you for the rest of the day. Confusing you every now and again when you stop to think if it was a dream or real? I was left feeling like that but, I seemed pretty sure that this affair was happening. I may have completely made-up extras to fill in the gaps, but I felt content that Daniel's actions laid the baseline. From my point of view anyway.

The days ahead became even darker, I felt lonelier. I became withdrawn from life and more obsessed with Daniel's infidelity. I felt sick. I felt pissed off. I felt hurt.

I was betrayed and I was living my actual nightmare. My worst fears were becoming reality and there was no way I was strong enough to run from the monsters within. Not this time anyway.

A few more days of me sat cooking on a low heat, the poison that was running through my veins was almost ready to ping. My very own potion! I called it 'shit is going to get messy potion'. With a dash of anger, a splash of fear, and a shit load of paranoia, I was brewing the ultimate health hazard concoction.

Daniel was still working late and going for his walks while I sat trying not to boil over and ruin my carpet. I really was trying so hard to keep my shit together, but still, I could see my paranoid behaviour pushing Daniel further and further away from me. Even though I was witnessing my actions rip apart my marriage like a hungry wolf, the pain was real. I was hungry for the truth. I just did not know what I was supposed to do, or how I was supposed to do it. I knew acting a little less paranoid would help, but how? My mind or body would not allow this. My mind wanted to fuck me over while my body wanted to lay down and let it happen.

I loved him so much, my heart feels like it was bleeding, but I also hated how I feel at this moment. The fear of losing him was immense, I doubt I could survive on my own, without him. I needed him in my life so much, so why could I not just show him how much I adored him? Time was ticking down until the day he went out for a permanent walk, or just stopped coming home from work. I needed to back off and try to fix this, somehow.

I sat most of that day trying to work out how I could make things better but got nowhere. I'm not even sure if Daniel knew what I thought I knew. I mean I'm content with the fact he understands how much I hate Janet, but does he understand why? I do not even think I fully understand why I hate her so much. I just know I do. I do remember though during one of my therapy sessions Daniel talked about how I just sat on my chair not doing or saying anything, while in my head I was fighting a war. Maybe it was like that now? I felt life was so chaotic, but could Daniel see that? I was not running around screaming or banging my head off the walls, and I did not recall telling him.

As the evening approached, I had decided to try and supress all negative feelings while pushing out some positive ones. This proved to be more difficult than I anticipated. It was like having constipation within. I could feel the feelings were there, they just needed more energy to push out than the negative ones. If only there were laxatives for feelings, I guess that's what wine is for. Verbal diarrhoea is something I could do without right now.

Once Daniel got home from work, he jumped straight in the shower. I thought I would go upstairs and sit on the bed to wait for him to finish. Maybe once he was done, I could ask how his day had been or ask if he would like me to make him some food. Baby steps!

So, I sat on the bed waiting, trying not to think about anything, just looking around the room as if it was brand new. I had a pretty nice room, that rug really went well with the curtains. Things were going so well until I spotted that Daniel had left his phone on the bedside table.

I just sat and staired at his phone for a minute before my head decided to think hey, why don't you check the phone? I started to feel strange. It was a strange feeling mixed up of nerves and desperation.

As I sat and thought about it, I decided no, I couldn't do that. That would be like taking a sledgehammer to our trust, and if Daniel were to catch me searching his phone, he would be upset that I didn't trust him. But what if the phone held evidence that proved my paranoia right? Could I actually be able to handle the shock? Did I even want to know the truth if it hurts so much? I could be proven wrong. It was highly possible I had made the whole affair up, leaving Daniel an innocent victim of my self-doubt. None of that mattered by the end, because Daniel had finished his shower before I could decide the best form of action to take. Probably for the best.

Before too long he was ready to leave for his walk. Out of nowhere I said, "I will come and walk with you, it will be nice to get out together." I am not going to lie, I was expecting at least some sort of happiness from him. I mean I was not expecting cartwheels and party streamers, but I wasn't expecting him to look disappointed either.

As his face filled with awkwardness he kindly replied with, "I won't be long, I just need to clear my head." Then he left the room before I had the chance to think of a comeback.

The panic I felt at that moment shot through my body like a defibrillator shocking life back into my soul. With one shot of adrenaline, I was sent straight into craze mode. I shouted, "Daniel please stop." As I chased him down the stairs. Daniel continued to get ready for his walk and sat down to put his trainers on while acting as if I was invisible. All I kept saying was, "Please Daniel! Let me come with you! It will be good for us, please don't leave." As I then followed him into the kitchen. I stood in front of the refrigerator door stopping him from getting his water bottle out. All the time I was on repeat, "Please Daniel." I pleaded so hard for him to stay while he was trying to force open the door of the refrigerator for his bottled water.

Daniel eventually gave in and shouted, "Fuck this," right in my face, I could feel his breath! But the second them words left his mouth I bolted for the back door. Knowing he was going to leave I tried to block his exit. Daniel walked over, grabbed me by both of my shoulders, pulled me away from the kitchen door then left.

I literally did not know what to do. I felt destroyed. I ran from one room to the other crying in panic until I eventually fell into a heaped mess on the living room floor. Daniel had gone for many walks without me so why was this time any different? I had used up 99% of my energy trying not to chase after him and after a big scream and a lot of tears I had no choice but to retreat to my bed, alone.

I eventually heard Daniel come back into the house. I lay there for a while hoping he would come upstairs to look for me or to see if I was ok, but he didn't. He stayed downstairs where he must have slept until he left for work the next morning.

CHAPTER 14.
<u>BROKEN TOMB.</u>

It had been a trying few days since the kitchen incident. Without two words spoken since that day, Daniel and I had started to live like two separate people. I couldn't speak for Daniel, but my heart was broken. Not only had I let him down by being me, but the girls also. Daniel's routine consisted of work, visiting the girls, showering then sleep, oh and his walks in-between. My daily routine was much simpler. I sit, think and sleep, all in a day's work.

As I sat swinging on my pedestal by my little worn-out thread, all I had left was my memories. I'm not sure what happened to me that evening in the kitchen, but I no longer lived in the now. I would relive the days I met Daniel, or the days I had taking care of my babies. They were such bright happy days, full of colour and laughter. Now and again my thoughts would wonder a little too far from the past. Edging closer to the present, the bright happy colours faded to grey, while the laughter turned to cries, the home full of love became an empty shadowy grave filled with life I have lost. I was officially entering the final stages of my battle to keep my mentality.

As I mentioned at the beginning, we all have life pockets. But what I did not mention was how we end up after our pockets have burst and our heads have exploded. Just like any unkept mess, the piles only get bigger. We then start to attract unwanted visitors. Picture our minds like a kitchen. We fill the cupboards week after week, only cleaning them out once maybe twice a year. They get full, the door gets tired with non-stop opening, then one day the door falls off exposing your shit to the world. We then either sort the shit or carry on like nothing is wrong. We, of course, continue to fill up our kitchen covering all the sides to the point there was no room to move, make food, or drinks. It drags you down. You stop taking out the rubbish as it feels like a never-ending battle. Then our kitchen starts attracting bugs or rats, making everything a thousand times worse. We have now found ourselves buried alive in our kitchen tomb. Now we have entered the final stages where we decide our fate. I am almost sure our fate has already been decided but we could cling on a little longer and drag out the inevitable.

Not everyone was destined for the same ending. Some of us may fight a little longer, clean up a little and fight some more. Very few of us are able to climb out of the crap continuing to live above it.

But then there are people like me, unable to fight anymore. If I felt I had something to fight for then I may have braved the climb, but I don't. Instead, I chose to get comfortable and embrace the tomb I now called home.

I felt I had made the right choice at this point. Prolonged fighting was only hurting the people I love, plus if I am honest, I was fucking tired of shit. This way I could live out the rest of my days in imaginative peace. The one good thing about being hidden amongst your own shit, is that you are surrounded by visual aids to keep the good times alive in your mind, even if you feel they have ended.

You may be be thinking what is the difference between the shit we have now, than the shit we had then? Well, that's easy. Your head has exploded out everything, making no room for any more therefore the present or future no longer matter. Clinging to the past is all we have left at this point which is why I was content for half my days. See, I play out my own story over and over, reliving the good, the best and even the worst times. I even throw in a few new stories that I have made up along the way.

Like this one time me and Daniel took the girls to the beach. It was such a lovely day we thought we would tell the girls that we had an appointment then surprise them with the beach. They were so happy running around as I chased them with a bucket of water, while Daniel sat down setting out our picnic lunch. Totally made up. But a nice memory nevertheless. I leave out the part where I really hate beaches. The smell, the people and definitely the sand. I had started to relive my life every day however real it was. Imaginative bliss.

It had now been a few days since the kitchen altercation and no words had been exchanged between me and Daniel. That day must have been the moment my head exploded because since then I have been hidden in my tomb.

This day in particular, Daniel arrived home a little earlier than he usually did. He did not rush to the shower but instead made a brew, then sat down in the living room in front of me. With no time to spare Daniel looked at me and said, "Sam, we need to talk."

Well, all I could think was that it was about time. Let's get over the kitchen incident, move on like it never happened. I had enough in me to turn and look at him all the while I was thinking how nice it would be to hear how my girls were doing. But then, somehow looking at Daniel's face opened the door of my tomb.

Like a brick in the face, I was forced back into the present time. Maybe it was not the girls he wants to tell me about. Or move past our kitchen fight. What if this was the day, he would leave me? Surely if he was leaving the effort of coming home early would be pointless. Maybe he was finally ready to admit his love for fucking Janet. So many things running around my head at top speed. Unable to cling to a single thought the panic was building.

"Sam, please! This is serious. You need to listen!"

As I tipped my head to the side to drain out all the thoughts, I managed to reply, "Ok." It was not much by I tried.

"I've been thinking. I feel it is best we sell the house."

MOTHER FUCKER! FUCK YOU DANIEL! Yeah, I never said that, but my head strongly thought it.

"I have spoken with your mum, and she agrees it might be best if you go home to her and get better."

For the first time in a long while, I was too stunned to even think.

"I know it is a lot to take in, Sam. I am going to grab a shower and give you some space. I do love you, you know that, don't you?".

I may not have been able to speak but I kept my eyes on that fucker. I watched him leave the room, I even continued to watch him through the walls and ceiling. On the outside I may have looked like a crazy lady following an invisible thing around my house with evil eyes, but on the inside, I was sending some badass vibes threw my glare hoping Daniel could feel my anger with every step he took.

Eventually I gave up the evil eyes, it became pointless and honestly my eyes started to hurt. Instead, I just sat there, like a car with a flooded engine, I was at a standstill. I tried my best to make sense of things and get my air to fuel ratio back to a usual balance and get going again. It was just not happening, well not as quickly as I needed it to.

Daniel finished his shower, gave me a little smile as he set off for his walk. I will add at this point that Daniel's smile instantly dried out my spark plugs. And no, not because it was a ray of sunshine. Or because the love soaked up all bitterness. But because he had pissed me the fuck off. Like a boiling kettle bursting, I was mad.

Why did he have to come home? Why could he not have left me locked away in my tomb, forever. I was away with the fairies and may not have even noticed he had left. What a fucking dick! Stupid fucking dick! Never in a million years did I even think Daniel could upset me this much! And then to piss off out for a walk! Oh, fuck this! I am going after the fucker!

As I left the house, slamming the door behind me, I saw Mrs. Jenner on her front lawn. Before she had chance to speak, I just looked at her, held up my hand and said, "Not right now!" I then stormed off like a boss. As I got halfway around the block, I started to realise that I never actually asked Daniel where he went for his walks, so I was basically walking blind. What the fuck am I supposed to do now? It was probably best I never caught up with him. I could have pulled a muscle busting out some ninja moves on him.

I made it back home and Mrs. Jenner was still in her garden, pulling up weeds or something. Well at least pretending to. I think she was just loitering in hope to see some drama. As I walked up my garden path, I saw her stand up. So, I shouted, "HI," in some weird creepy but happy voice and kept walking.

As I got back behind the doors of my tomb, it just felt different. Daniel was not home yet, but that's nothing new. It was as if my home had become contaminated or something. The safe feeling, I had before has gone. It was as if by the scruff of my neck I was dragged out from my tomb and plonked on the top. I did not choose to be on the top of the pile. I wanted to be buried. What the hell has just happened? I felt like a little mouse burrowing back into his safe place, only to find someone else has moved in.

As I sat in my chair dwelling on the fact my retirement plan has been disturbed, I saw Daniel making his way to our garden. He must have only got two feet on the path when Mrs. Jenner popped up from behind the fence, like a jack in the box. Fuck knows what they were talking about, but my guess was she was filling Daniel in on my angry power walk. Given how Mrs. Jenner likes to exaggerate, I am surprised Daniel came in the house at all.

Luckily for him, I had calmed down lots by the time he had got into the house. To be honest all I could do at this point was sit and try to figure out why my home felt different. I had all the same things, and nothing has been moved or taken. It just felt odd.

I finally reached a conclusion, it was all Daniel's fault because my house no longer felt safe. Well, he did send a bomb crashing through my tomb with his lets sell the house bullshit, cracking the bond we had together right down the middle. Like a leaking bucket, it all just seemed useless. It was morning now and I had no idea what Daniel did when he got home or where he was now.

As I braced myself for another day of thinking, then sorting, then thinking again I decided I missed my life pockets. I know carrying around pockets full of shit was a workout but at least I knew where shit was and where to put it. My pockets were beyond repair and my tomb, well, that's just open to the public now. Maybe I had hit the very last stage. Is this really make or break time? I guess I could cling on a little longer. It is never too late to climb out of the mess I call life.

I continued the day fighting with my mixed

emotions. One minute I had given up, the next I would rise like a champion taking back what is mine, while in between crying like a baby that has lost her favourite toy. I had to change tactics, this is getting me nowhere.

Ok, Sam get your head out your arse and think! Think about all of them snobby people walking around your house, deciding if I was good enough for them. Touching your stuff! Painting over your memories! Dusting off your good times! That was it, the break I needed to rise like a bear woken from his hibernation! I was not leaving without a fight! No one was touching my stuff!

By this point I had no clue how much, if any time had passed since Daniel mentioned the selling of the house. I do know that I woke up to April knocking on the door. Apparently, Daniel thought it would be a good idea, again to go behind my back, and contact April. Do not get me wrong, April was a nice girl and probably good at her job, it was just the circumstances were rotten. I guess she would not be here, sitting on my chair if shit was good.

She said, "HI," before parking her butt on Daniels chair. Daniel being the coward he had turned into, let April in then ran off to work.

"Hey Sam, how are you doing?"

I tried not to be completely rude, so I just sat and shrugged my shoulders. It was better than nothing, plus more than she had gotten from me in the past.

"Daniel has told me that he has mentioned to you that things may be better if you go and stay with your mum? Is that right?"

Yeah, it's fucking right! Again, I never spoke that out loud, but my face surely got the message across.

"He feels you may benefit from my visits to help you understand what is to happen and when? Is that something you are willing to try?"

At this point I had lost all sense and feeling. I did not even know what to think. Surely I was not expected to just sit and wait for someone to move in my home, then rip the rug out from underneath me? Well, that was not happening! I liked this rug! The rug was mine!

Then unexpectedly out of nowhere I said, "Please leave." Yeah, I know! I was shocked too, and it was in a nice voice, so I was not a complete monster. April talked a little more before she left and honestly, I had switched off once I asked her to leave so no idea what her last words before she left were. I did need a plan though!

So, I made a brew and lit a smoke, and I did not even go to the back door! I then nearly passed out as I took the first drag of my smoke. In my defence I had been sitting in that chair doing fuck all for months, it must have just been an old habit resurfacing. Getting back to the matter at hand, I need a plan. What if I just ran around screaming anytime someone knocked on my door? That could work although people only seem to knock on my door when I was either asleep or my butt had just hit the toilet seat. I could give the Tweeds a constant supply of booze. Just as an apology for punching her stupid face. That would scare the street away, I would have to speak to them though. I don't think I was that desperate yet. What if, seeing as I felt numb inside maybe I could pretend I was fine? That way I could try to trick myself into thinking all was good. Like teaching a baby to walk, I just needed to teach myself how to live. Worth a try. I did just get up off my chair and make a brew so how hard could it be.

Well, it was not the best plan in the world, but it was all I had so, fuck it! Let the show begin.

CHAPTER 15.
SHOW TIME!

As I was progressing through day one of my plan, things were going ok. Well, I said day one but technically I only decided my plan halfway through the day and now the clock was touching five. I had pretty much finished the day.

After my busy day of planning, I decided I had earned the right to sit in my chair and chill.

It was not long before Daniel pulled up in his car after his long day at work, or whatever the fuck he did during the day. As he made his way through the door, I was going to tackle this as if I had a loaded gun. I shot first with, "Hey, how was your day?"

He looked a little freaked out but replied, "Not bad."

Quick on my heels I hit back with, "And how were the girls?"

As he turned away, he said, "They were good." My gun was running low on ammo, but I managed to take a third shot.

"Would you like a brew?"

As Daniel stopped in his tracks, he turned and said, "I see April's visit went well." I was a little wounded but still manage to shoot back with an it was ok. Daniel made some humming sound as he continued with his journey to the shower. Yeah, I was a little more than just wounded but plodded on. I made myself and Daniel a brew then sat down to wait for him to finish.

Once he finished his shower, he was downstairs and ready for his walk. I suggested we stay in and watch a film, but Daniel did not seem interested. He then downed his brew before sitting down to put his trainers on. I had one bullet left, do I save it? Or give it my best shot? I decided to aim high and take the shot, so I beat Daniel to the door.

As I opened the door I said, "It will be nice to have a walk together, don't you think?"

Before I managed to get both feet out of the door I was shot in the back. "What exactly are you trying to achieve here Sam?"

That really was a near fatal shot, I slowly turned to face my attacker. While gasping for air I quietly said, "Please Daniel, I'm trying," The look on Daniel's faces was empty, emotionless. Is that really how empty I looked over the past year? Cold and empty. He just looked so different. His eyes appeared darker with an emotionless stare. I just felt nothing from him. No love, no hate just nothing.

As a tear run down the side of my cheek, Daniel brushed past me muttering, "I haven't got time for this!" Wow! Not only did he shoot me in the back but he stepped over my dying body. If I had any chance of making this work, then I need to start smoking again. I headed back in the house to revise my plan while Daniel was out.

Well, he was not completely ignoring me so that's a positive. Surely I had not been so bad towards him. Yeah, I had been neglectful and maybe built a wall between us called "Janet" but other than that, all I did was sit in silence. Maybe he needed love? Maybe if I was more persistent with my plan then he would come around. I just needed to show him I did love him, and that I was sorry for how I had been. This was no longer about my home, I needed to also help Daniel.

By the time I had my shower and got in my comfy clothes, Daniel was home. He sat down on his chair, took off his trainers, then sat and stared at the television. I sat and waited a few minutes before saying, "How about that film?"

He made no effort whatsoever to answer me properly. He just let out a big sigh, shook his head then said, "Not tonight."

Wow! This was really getting on my nerves. Was I seriously this annoying? As the night went on all Daniel did was stare at the television watching crap. I do not even think he was really watching it as he seemed to be in another world. Not like a pocket bursting world but a world better than he thought this one was.

Daniel eventually stood up saying, "I'm going to bed," and just left the room. He did not seem depressed. He seemed sulkier than anything. Sulking like a child that had been made to stay home instead of being allowed out to play. Well, I was not admitting defeat just yet, so I turned off the television and followed him up to bed.

Once I got upstairs to the bedroom Daniel was already in bed. He was sat up playing on his phone, so I popped to the toilet for a wee before getting into bed. As I got into bed next to him, he put his phone on the bedside table then laid down to sleep. Well, it was clearly not sex he was missing. I disappointedly whispered good night as I lay down ready for the night. Seen as he never answered me, I thought I would give it one last shot before he fell asleep, so I told him I loved him. This time he said, "I love you," back so I felt a little better.

Ten maybe fifteen minutes into bedtime Daniel's phone lit up the room. I have no idea if he had a text message or a phone call, his phone was on silent, but he quickly flipped his phone over to hide the screen.

"Are you not going to answer that?" I whispered.

Daniel let out such a big sigh before snatching his phone off the side and stomping off to the bathroom. I chose to keep quiet and wait for him to get back.

When he returned, he said, "It was Dave from work, moaning about shift change." He then stuffed his phone under his pillow and got back in bed.

I was determined to get comfortable in bed and not think too much into this. The paranoia pocket was no longer on my hip. Plus, I had been distant for so long that maybe this was how Daniel was now. Or maybe he just wanted to kill two birds with one stone. I mean if you must get up to check your phone you may as well use the time to go for a pee as well. It was possible, I guess.

With nothing left to do apart from stare at the back of Daniel's head, all I could feel was sadness. Sadness that the man next to me may no longer be Daniel. The feeling of comfort I used to get by sleeping next to him had drained away. He did not seem to hate me or love me, he seemed distracted, and I was not the distraction. Tonight, I felt like I was nothing more than a fly getting too close just to be whacked away. I know it was my own fault, I had not been the best wife or mum, in fact I had not even been a nice person full stop. Without making too many excuses for myself, none of this was entirely my fault. Yeah, I could have been a stronger person, but no one had full control once their mental health started to slip. It was no different than running down a slippery slope, you can try and regain control but until you hit the bottom, it seems pointless.

I don't know for sure if I had lost Daniel at this point, but I did know I wanted him back. And my girls. I guess I had to walk the painful path of fixing bridges. It would be hard, and I knew that. But it seemed the closer I tried to get to Daniel the more distance it caused between us. It is a bit like when I was young, trying to shake off Jessica because I had more things important to me to be doing, only in this scenario I was Jessica and Daniel was me.

As the days passed me by, nothing much had changed. I was still managing to keep up my positive, happy appearance despite Daniel not seeming to care. The future was looking a little brighter as I had managed to have a conversation with Daniel about the girls coming home. I say conversation, but it was mainly me being lectured by Daniel with, "It will take more than a few good days," and "It won't happen overnight," bullshit. He did agree to start bringing them home on weekends, but only on a trial basis. It was better than nothing, but I still couldn't help but feel the shame. What kind of mother was I to lose rights to see my own children. More so, not even realise until they were gone! My poor babies.

I really couldn't wait to see my girls, I really was

craving them so much. I wondered if they had grown any or changed their hair. I wondered if they miss me. What if they didn't? What if they were disappointed in me? Or never wanted to see me again? I couldn't blame them for any negative feelings towards me, I could only try and make it up to them. Somehow. As now was only Tuesday I had to keep myself together for them. I was so scared something would come up, leaving me waiting another week just to hug my girls.

Keeping my head together would be challenging as Daniel seemed to be resentful towards me. I was starting to feel like he was gutted I was appearing to get better. It was like I had ruined his plans, whatever they were. I just assumed he wanted me to get better, for him and for the girls. Could I possibly be wrong? What if I was right before? And he did want me out of the picture to live happily with fucking Janet.

I missed my pockets, shit seemed easier to sort out when I had dedicated pockets to file it in. I think deep down I knew fine well what his problem was, but I couldn't afford to fall again.

Wednesday arrived and I was still together, very confused but together. Not being able to keep a single thought in my mind for longer than a minute seemed to help but also caused more confusion. I used to always wish my life pockets would bugger off, but now I was beginning to understand their purpose in life. Without my pockets I was unable to sort through my feelings, my mind couldn't seem to make sense of which issue should feel what emotions, leaving me feeling nothing. My memories no longer felt real, they just felt like stories. And when a new issue arose, it just passed through my head like a breeze. Did this mean I could no longer store new memories? Or feel the old ones? There was only one thing I could think of that will make me feel any sort of emotion and that was my girls.

Making it through my days got easier but the night times were a different fight altogether. The way Daniel had started to act was forcing me into a pit of paranoia. I was balancing on a rope ready to fall any minute. Determined I was going to keep my balance for the girls, I was eventually going to be knocked over the edge by Daniel's weird behaviour. You would think that revisiting a place for the second time would be easier, wouldn't you? Well, that was bullshit because the second time was definitely worse.

As I sat pondering in the deadly pit of paranoia, I became once again lost. Lost in a mixture of old and new feelings without the head power to make sense of any of it, I was sent deeper in the canyon of crap.

I think I needed to check his phone. Break my own rule and find out what he was hiding, but how? Or when? I should have checked it before, when I had the chance. At least it would have been over by now. He has become so protective over his phone since I got my sight back, he has even started to sleep with it underneath his pillow. I was surprised he did not carry it around during the day in a locked briefcase handcuffed to his wrist. I could try and follow him while he was out for his daily walk? Stalker style? Maybe not as that was just crying out desperation. I could try go for a walk with him. I know it did not work last time but what if I was more persistent this time, ignoring what he said and just followed him anyway. Well, there was only one of two ways it could go, he would either get upset again or give in and we'd have a nice walk, together. I guess time would tell.

So, I spent most the day preparing myself for a hopefully nice walk with Daniel. I did my hair, put on nice clothes and even stretched to a little makeup. Well, I felt nice even if Daniel blew me off later plus, I got to see my girls tomorrow, so I was feeling pretty good. I was feeling that good, I thought I would sit out in the back garden while I waited for Daniel to arrive home.

Eventually I heard his car pull into the driveway. Now was the time to pump up my courage and pack away the paranoia. Daniel did not even bother to say hi or check if I was home, he just went straight upstairs to the shower. So, I thought if I was going to get through this in one piece, I had best start doing more, thinking less. Maybe if I go upstairs and say hi or ask how his day has been could give me a little indicator of how the night may go.

As I walked into the bedroom ready to play the caring wife, I had quickly noticed he had dumped his keys, wallet and mobile phone onto the bed before jumping into the shower. I did not speak, I just silently sat on the edge of the bed. I could not help but feel I needed to check his phone. Once I picked up his phone all tonight's plans may be ruined. He drove me to this, leaving not many options. Why would he act so secretly if he had nothing to hide? To be fair to him he was acting more protectively weird than secret.

Well, now or never. I picked up Daniels mobile phone and swiped right to unlock the screen. For someone so protective you would have thought he would have a pin or fingerprint to unlock it, at least some security. As I sat there just staring at the phone, it just felt wrong. I felt so frightened. It was like I was committing an offense! Was I going to be hung for this criminal activity? Maybe I should put the phone down and not dig my grave any deeper. I then noticed he had an unread text message and decided no one liked a shallow grave anyways, so I investigated further.

As the text message was from "Dave" I just assumed it was the same Dave that was moaning the other night about shift changes at work, so I scrolled down to check out the other names. There was not a single text from Janet, so that was a plus. Once I got to the bottom of Daniel's text messages, I scrolled back up to the top to look again at "Dave's" message. Without clicking to read the full text message I could see it started with, "Tonight?" but the rest was hidden. Shall I read it? I really needed to think this through. It could just be another moan about shifts.

As I decided that I had already dug my grave I may as well jump in, feet first so I opened the message. Well, there was no going back now, the message was open, I may as well read it. So, I did. How would I even explain this to Daniel? "Oh, what! This is not my phone!." I doubt he would believe I was that stupid. Anyways no point worrying about it now the deed is done.

As I began to read the text message from Dave, I felt an instant sickness consume my entire body! The text message read, tonight? Same place? XX.

Did this mean Daniel was not walking alone? That is if he was walking at all! It does make a little more sense now why he did not want me to walk with him. But why hide this? As I read more of the text messages some points started to make more sense while others caused more confusion.

I really wish I had never pick up Daniel's stupid phone! Maybe not knowing the truth was for the best. The things I was reading that was written by Daniel was just nasty. It was hard to digest! He was saying things like, 'the stupid bitch is on one again' and 'I fucking hate being here! With her!' Is this how Daniel really felt about me? How many more lies had he been telling me? Dave's replies were not any easier to chew either! 'Just leave! Come stay here with me xx.'

The more I read the more "Dave" sounded more like a "Davina". Why is Dave putting kisses on the end of every text message?

Why was Daniel making me out to be such a horrible bitch? I know I had been ill, but that was not my fault! Any illness does not and should not define the person you are. If there was a supermarket that sold new brains, I would have bought a dozen. I feel devastated beyond words at this moment.

Eventually Daniel had finished his shower. He marched straight towards me snatching the phone from my hands. He was so upset, I had never seen him this upset before. He just started to shout, "I cannot cope with this Sam! Your trust issues! You! You are ruining my life! The kids life!"

I did feel my heart crack down the middle listening to his rant, but I still managed to ask, "Are you seeing someone else, Dan?"

He replied with another rant about how he couldn't cope with my paranoid head or my clinginess, but I stopped him mid-way by saying, "Please! I need to know?"

Well, those words were like gasoline on a fire! He screamed so loud at me, "NO!!" and punched the bedroom door on his way out.

I was well and truly lost this time. What was I supposed to do? Wasn't it me that was supposed to be upset? He was the one keeping secrets, not me. Why was I the one sitting here crying for being told off, like a child.

As I sat on my bed and cried for a good hour my makeup ended up as scary as my life, and my nice hair was as greasy as Daniel's secret life. I just did not know what I was supposed to do, or who to even trust now. What if Daniel was right and all this was in my head? Could I even trust myself after past experiences? How was I supposed to be able to figure this out if I had no clue myself what was real and what was not? I mean, I feel no different now than I would waking up from a nightmare so how the fuck am I to know if my head was functioning as well as I thought it was. What if, in reality I am still sat in my chair, staring at the window daydreaming up all this shit? Surely a daydream could not hurt this much inside.

I eventually got off my bed to go downstairs. Daniel was in the living room on his phone. As I looked at him, I could not help but cry and tell him how sorry I was. Daniel responded quickly to my sorrowful cry with, "Do you want me to fuck off? No, you don't! So stop!"

When did he turn so cruel? Never had I seen or heard Daniel like this. Like a little told off puppy I sat in my chair and silently cried. No matter how hard I tried to stop the tears they just kept pouring, like a tap with a constant drip. I was so sorry for what I had done but also very confused, I was devastated.

Eventually Daniel must have gotten sick of me sitting and crying as he just got up and went to bed, giving me the space to cry, on my own.

CHAPTER 16.
THE TRUTH.

I tried putting all the pieces together, but I was left with one that didn't fit. Dave. If Daniel was having an affair, then the showering before going for a walk makes more sense, right? Because normal people shower after exercise. But I really do not think Daniel was attracted to men! But what I do think is Dave wrote text messages like a woman, or a man I love.

The more I sat and thought about this the more desperate for the truth I became. I know me, and me would not survive seeing Daniel with another person. Whether it be male or female, not everyone would survive this.

I needed to know the truth. There was no crazy like the crazy you got from not knowing, so I made my way to the bedroom. It had gotten pretty late so Daniel was asleep. Like the crazy bitch I was, I just stood there at the foot of the bed and stared at him. So many things passed through my head. Did he really love me? You would not talk that way about a person you love. I know I have called him a fucker a few times but never out loud, or to a person. He just looked like a stranger. A stranger that I felt so much love for, that the thought of him leaving frightened me.

As Daniel turned over in bed, I felt instantly nervous. Luckily, he didn't wake. Imagine after all I had done tonight, and he woke up and saw me just standing there!

As I was about to give up the creepy bedtime stare, I noticed his phone peeping out from his pillow. So, I took it and rushed downstairs like a child at Christmas.

I remember sitting in my chair at this point thinking what now? I really did not think this through. Well, actually I did not think at all. Shit! Just shit! is this the be all, end all moment I was destined to reach?

Before I knew it, I had pressed call Dave, and the phone was against me ear. I was really fucking up this time! But still, I was seeing this thing through. As the phone was ringing, I started to panic. What if it is Dave? Or even worse! Not Dave!

The phone eventually rang off and the call was diverted to an answer machine. And not Dave's answer machine either!

"Hi, you have reached Susan, leave a message."

I was legit sick in my mouth before quickly ending the call. Soon after I had ended the call Dave, I mean Susan rang back. Should I face this demon head on? Or pretend nothing has happened? Well, it would be pointless pretending nothing had happened as I hold the evidence in my hand. Luckily the phone had stopped ringing before I had a chance to make the drastic decision.

As I sat back in my chair feeling a little relief, Daniel received a text message. It was from Dave, and it read 'are you ok? Xx'. I thought about it for a minute and decided seen as I was already in my grave I may as well cover myself over and finish the job. So, I texted back, 'this is Sam. Who is this?' It was not long before the reply came through. It was Susan! Who the actual fuck is Susan! And why is she saved as Dave in Daniel's phone.

Shit was starting to get real, so I just came straight out with it. 'Are you and Daniel seeing each other?'

Her reply was the best! 'Yeah! What's it to you!' The cheeky bitch! Who the fuck was this cow! Oh, I was raging! My body started to shake from my head to my toes. I had literally felt my heart snap into two pieces and fall out my arse. I think I was going into shock! Then another text message came through.

'Look I know its shit to find out like this, but you brought this on yourself! You have ruined his life! Do the honourable thing and let him be happy! We love each other, move on for fuck's sake.'

I was furious. Who the fuck is she to tell me what I had done and what I should do. She did not know me! I doubt she even knew Daniel properly! And she wanted to talk about being honourable! The tramp!

I raced up my stairs faster than I had ever managed before and kicked open the bedroom door. As Daniel jumped up from his sleep I launched the phone right at him, called him an arsehole then left the room.

While Daniel was left with his phone catching up on the latest gossip I retreated to my chair. I cannot even begin to explain how I felt at that moment, all I knew was that I needed to throw up. If my heart had not fallen out my arse earlier then I would be damn sure it was forcing its way up through my mouth. I was just thoughtless, empty. It was as if I had been hit on the head from behind and too dazed to work out what had just happened.

Time ticked away until I heard Daniel starting to get ready for work. The sick feeling inside me bubbled to the top. I was not sure if I was scared or extremely nervous. Was my life about to walk out the door and not come back? He could feel bad and tell me how sorry he was. Either way I couldn't let him leave without knowing for sure so, I headed upstairs to face the truth.

The first words to leave my mouth was, "Please stay home," Looking at how fast Daniel turned to look at me after just saying them three words, it was safe to assumed that this was ending in disaster.

He screamed so loud, "I can't breathe anymore! Sam, you are suffocating me with your constant shit!"

Well, he was being a bit dramatic, but I screamed back anyways. I made it perfectly clear that if he was cheating then to just confess, then maybe we can move past it. Oh, he was having none of it! Saying "Dave" was messing around and thought it was funny and the only problem was me with my paranoid thoughts. Yeah, well, I may have paranoid thoughts, but does Dave really sound that feminine?

As Daniel left the room to head downstairs, the panic took over my body. I instantly felt that if Daniel left now, he would not come back so I grabbed a hold of his shirt. I begged so much for him not to leave me and stay home. I told him we can forget this had even happened and go back to normal. I held him so tight, I was so desperate for him to stay. He eventually pushed me off. As I fell back on to the stairs, Daniel got so close to my face! He screamed until his face turned purple, "NO," then left for work.

I stayed sat on the stairs crying for a while before I replayed the conversation I had with Susan again in my head. Just the thought of her gave me the motivation to get up. This was not finished! Not yet! I got in my car and drove to the place Daniel worked.

As I pulled up outside the car park of his work, I instantly spotted his car, he was here. In that building, with her probably. After I smoked a cigarette for courage, I opened the door to the reception office. I had a quick glance around and saw nothing unusual. As I made my way to the receptionist, I became more confident. Without thinking I asked for Dave. It was no surprise when she informed me, they had nobody by the name Dave working there, but they did have a Daniel.

Well so far, I have not learnt anything new, apart from I was not as brain dead as I thought I was. I was just about to ask for Daniel when a door open and out came a giggling blond woman followed by Daniel. After seeing what I definitely assumed was Susan, another piece of me died inside. Janet was way better looking and less fake.

I was then ushered outside by a panicked Daniel. The shock of seeing me there sent his face white. As soon as I had both feet outside Daniel quietly asked me why I was there. I sure enough asked if the giggling blow-up doll that i just saw him with was Susan.

Daniel whispered, "Yes! She is called Susan and no! we are not doing this now!" As he was still pushing me towards my car. I could not help but cry out in desperation as I told him how sorry I was and that if he just came back home, we could talk. Daniel continued pushing me closer to my car. He just did not want to listen to me.

"Daniel please! Just stop and listen to me! We can move past this!"

It seemed clear Daniel did not want to move past anything unless it was me. I just could not accept that though as I continued to push back. I told him everything I could think of to make him come home. As I edged closer to my car the words just poured out my mouth.

"I am getting better! I will go therapy and take my pills from Dr. Khan every day! Just listen to me Daniel!"

He must have been listening as his reply was, "It is too late Sam! You had your chances! I cannot live like this anymore! Just go home!"

I had finally reached my car and with nowhere else to go apart from home, I dished out the final ultimatum. Family or staying at work, with Susan. I was not expecting us to click our fingers, and everything will be better, I just thought we should at least try. All Daniel was doing at this point was shaking his head.

As I sat in my car and rolled down my window, I tried one last time before I left. I pleaded for him to please choose me. Choose our family, everything we had together. I told him again how better I have been lately and am trying my hardest. The last words Daniel said to me before he walked off back into work was, "Your hardest is not good enough!" That cut deep! In fact, I think those words cut all the way through, leaving no nerve unharmed.

Somehow, I had made it home and the first thing I did was get into my bed. I cried so much. The thought of Daniel at work all cosy with Susan was burning me from the inside. How could he leave me so broken like he did not care? Even if you liked someone surely you would want to help them feel better. If he was so unhappy then who gave him the right to keep me in the dark? No matter how ill a person is, you should never live a lie. Especially a lie that only suits your own need.! If you want to see another person then fine, leave then do it! It is not so hard! Why drag it out, make things worse, it's just cruel.

As I turned over in my bed to face Daniel's side, I could instantly smell him. If I closed my eyes, I could pretend he was still here and not with her. So, I cried while sniffing Daniel's pillow like a weirdo for a few more minutes. The more I imagined Daniel with her, the more scared I became. I picked up my phone to ring him. Give him another chance to reconsider.

The more I rang him the quicker he was at rejecting my calls. After that, I must have sent him a dozen text messages asking him to just talk to me. He still did not care enough to answer. Is this really it for me? Have I officially lost everything?

I felt so frightened that I was unsure what to do while being so nervous as I did not know what my future was going to be like. Not only have I ruined my own life, but Daniel's as well. And what about my girls? Are they about to inherit prefilled pockets? On the day of their periods are they going to wake up to a special delivery! A box full of shit, nicely wrapped up and tied with a bow! With a side note reading "love mum".

I eventually gave up on the texting as I was practically talking to myself. I just laid down in my bed and cried some more. The amount I was missing Daniel was scary. How can you miss someone this much? Eventually my phone beeped, it was a text from Daniel. Maybe he just needed time to think and chose me after all. I started to feel a little more hopeful. He did take the time to message me back so I must be in his thoughts. Without getting too excited I open his message.

"Sam, I cannot do this anymore. I will come back home but only for my things. I am going to stay at my mums with the girls. The girls really do not need to see us fighting any more so I am sorry, but they will not be coming with me when I pick up my things."

The rage filled my body as I just let out the biggest scream. I just started to throw, smash or punch anything in sight. My head hurts, I could no longer breathe properly, I just lost control. I looked forward to seeing the girls. He fucking knew that!

They made me better! They helped me to keep on living! I fucking hated him! I hated Susan! I tried my best but that was not good enough! Why me!! Why fucking me!!!

The rest of the day from then on was a blur. I am not sure if I kept fighting my furniture like a champion or I passed out, I just knew Daniel was coming home soon.

CHAPTER 17.
IS THIS THE END? OR A NEW BEGINNING?

Isn't life funny? And people, well we are the beings that makes life. We lie, we cheat, none of us really follow the rules, we steal, we fight, we just hurt each other and ourselves. We still manage to somehow survive. It is a mess! We are a mess! There are some people with everything, then some with nothing. Some people want everything while some are happy to make do. I am one of the people that had everything but lost it all. I am one of those people that was destined to suffer no matter what happened and now I was suffering more than ever.

Waiting for Daniel to get here for his stuff was one of the worst waits I have ever had to endure. I had so many different feelings wiggling around my body but yet not one of them felt real. I was happy that I get to see him again while at the same time devastated, I would have to say goodbye for the second time today. I also felt extremely nervous for the fact I had no idea what later will bring and heartbroken for the fact that later would no longer bring my girls home.

Maybe if Daniel saw how much I missed him he might change his mind and choose me. Or take one look at the state of the house after my tantrum and walk back out. I had trashed the house! It was as messy as my life. I had smashed so many memories, broken a lot of good times.

As I found myself scuttering around the house trying to salvage what was left of my home, I had found myself at a point of denial. It was a strange feeling especially when less than a minute ago I was feeling so broken to breathe. I found myself pottering around the house as if nothing had happened. It was bizarre! It really was as if someone had hit the rewind on my life. I felt as sound as I did before Susan ruined everything! Stupid cow!

As the dreaded time was nearly upon me, I knew it would not be long now when Daniel called for his things. Seeing as I had not seen or spoke to him properly since our row this morning it all started to become quite daunting. I soon snapped out of denial mode as once again I was hit with the ton of bricks called realisation. This morning happened so fast, for me it did anyways. God only knows how long Daniel and Susan have been happening. Weeks? Months? I would not know because I was too ill and preoccupied with my head to notice!

What will I say when he arrives? "Hey! How was

your day of infidelity? Catch any diseases?" Was I supposed to be happy to see him or angry he had the cheek to come back? If I didn't want him to stay so much, I would have thrown his stuff outside. Like a scattered muddy mess and watch him pick up the pieces for a change.

With every car that passed my house I would feel sick with nerves. You would be surprised how many cars you can hear when you are waiting for a specific one. It is a lot. Two million cars later and Daniel had finally arrived. Nothing could have prepared me for the feeling I experienced when I saw him get out of his car. Nothing! It was excruciating! It was definitely something I had never experienced or wish to again.

As I stood there watching Daniel come through the door, I just froze. This could be the last time I ever see him. Why is this happening. How is this happening? My story was not supposed to end this way! Where was my happy ending? Is it not written in most books that people with troubled lives finally get their happy ending? Have I not suffered enough to earn one? Or cried enough to at least earn a reasonable ending? This is utter bullshit! I would be happy with any ending that does not involve Daniel leaving or my girls not being allowed to come home.

While I was stood frozen, Daniel had made his way upstairs to pack his things. But once I had thawed out I went up to take my front row seat and watch my life walk away. Daniel had dug out an old suitcase from under the bed to fill up with his things. It was heart-breaking to watch as he seemed a totally different Daniel than the one I knew and grew to love. As I watch the suitcase get fuller and fuller, I started to feel the panic set in. He was really doing this! He is actually going to leave! This was not a joke!

Tonight, was supposed to be nice. The girls were going to come around. We were going to cuddle, eat ice-cream and watch movies! Not fear I may never see them again while my life packs up his shit then leaves. The world was even more cruel than I thought.

Daniel's suitcase was practically full when I asked him to just sit down and talk to me. He did not even think, his answer was a straight away blunt, "No."

So, I started to shout. "After all these years, do you not think I at least deserve an explanation?" Daniel still did not want to engage in conversation with me. He was only bothered about collecting his things so, I stood right in front of him, and I yelled, "Just stop!" Like I was invisible, Daniel turned away continuing to collect stuff around me. I started to shout louder, "You cannot ignore me forever Daniel!"

Then his cold harsh reply hit me like a snowball in the face, "Sam! I am going to leave!" Ouch!

Seriously though what had I done so wrong to deserve this. Surely I deserved some explanation. I can and will accept full responsibility for my part played in this, but Daniel needs to accept his. This was not all my doing! No matter how much he wanted to shift the blame, he was not excused for his own wrong doings.

The more he was ignoring me the more riled I became. It was not a game! I was genuinely feeling this and I exploded! Everything came out! I just started to shout while following him around the house. I will give him credit where it was due because he did very well at keeping his cold hearted attitude and left me talking to myself.

Without any warning my mood flipped! I had gone from needing him to own up to his wrong doings and demanding answers to crying and begging for forgiveness. There was definitely nothing dignified about the way I am acting tonight, that's for sure. I cried so much my nose was dripping with snot! I begged so hard! All I wanted was him to sit down and talk to me or at least acknowledge I was there.

Daniel had just about gathered everything he needed to take with him when my mood switched back into fuck you and tell me everything mode. I was still on his tail like a tiger on the hunt, but he still did not seem to care! He shown me no remorse whatsoever, like my feelings meant nothing to him. His aura seemed lighter as if he was carrying less baggage. Well, his secret was out! I suppose that is the kind of secret that will weigh you down.

Once Daniel had everything he needed he then headed into the girl's room. I continued to follow him still shouting. "What the fuck are you doing in here?"

As he picked up one of Emily's jackets off her bed he said, "The girls have asked me to pick up a few things for them while I am here." I then snatched the jacket right out of his hands!

"Put it down! Do not touch my girl's stuff!" I was so upset.

Daniel said, "Sam! They have both asked me to bring them a few more things!"

My mood switched again! Only this time I turned into a crazed hoarder, and someone was taking away my things! Everything Daniel picked up, I took back off him. I had felt he had already taken enough from me, and the girls' things were all I have left that was of any importance to me.

It was not long before Daniel started to get annoyed with me constantly taking everything off him, he just started to grab all he could and shove it into a black bin liner. Once I started to feel he had grabbed as much as he was able, I then bolted to block the girl's bedroom door with my body. No way on earth was I letting him walk away with my girls' things.

"Put it all back!" I screamed so loud in his face while he was trying to get out the door.

"Get out my fucking way!" he screamed back.

Things started to get ugly quickly! There was so much shouting I doubt half of the shit said made any sense. The pushing and nudging got really heavy until I was finally overpowered by Daniel. He had managed to push me to the side and broke free from the girl's room.

By now I was in such a bad state I have no idea what came over me, as I jumped out the girls' room like the tiger finally catching its prey. I grabbed the bag with their things inside that Daniel had a hold of, trying my best to take them back. It was an instant tug of war match beentween Daniel and me. The bag did not last that long before it had ripped, scattering the girl's possessions all down the stairs.

As I fell to the floor, Daniel got so close to my face and said, "I hope you are happy now!"

Well actually no I was not! Why would I be happy! As I looked back into Daniel's eyes, I no longer knew him. All the love had gone. But for a slight moment I felt hate, proper genuine hate! My brain then started to wake up, he was the bad one! He took your girls! He was not going to stop until everything has been taken! He did this! He does not care! He was going to live happy, with my girls and their new mum! Susan!

Keeping it in mind that all these thoughts running through my head had only taken a second. One single second it took for my head to play out Daniel's story if I let him walk away! Why did he deserve a happy ending? Another split second later and Daniel was no longer standing in front of me. He was laying at the bottom of the stairs. I had pushed him!

I remember sitting at the top of the stairs just looking at Daniel's lifeless body, just lying there, so peacefully. I was not lying when I tell you I did feel some sense of relief that this was all over.

I assumed at this point people were expecting me to scream in panic for help, but I did not even shed a single tear from that moment on. I was broken. My head was finally allowed to withdraw back into my tomb. It had felt like my soul had finally been set free. I felt no pain, no anger, hey I could be dead for all I was aware! I was just happy living inside my head with the memories I have chosen. Me, Daniel and the girls were all together again, happy!

I could not tell you how long I sat on the top of the stairs, dreaming of everything nice before I was being forced back into reality. Suddenly, my dreams were being interrupted by so much noise. People started to scream, sirens had surrounded me. My dreams started to get darker as I could feel the force of someone pulling at me and shouting my name! It must have been a few days before I was fully able to wake up, not by choice either.

As I started to come around there were at least two people in the room with me. It was mostly a blur. A bit like when you are super tired and finally drift off to sleep, then someone decides they want to talk. You struggle to keep your eyes open causing reality to merge with your dreams. It was like that. The room was only small with a bed and a small, barred window you could barely see out of. One lady kept asking me if I knew where I was and if I knew why I was here. The other fellow was sat taking notes. I have no idea what he was noting down because I was lying on a bed, staring at the window saying nothing. They always give up eventually and left me to drift back into my tomb. They did pop back every so often to do their checks or to prod me back into the world of suffering, asking the same questions then bugger off back to their office. I was mostly left in peace.

This is my ending. May not be a happy one but I am no longer with it to care. Yes, I have lost everything, including my freedom, but I am no longer able to feel the suffering. My head is no longer capable of acknowledging anything else apart from my own happy memories. I may look like a person, who has suffered, who has caused suffering and who no longer lives in this world, but I am ok. I will live out the rest of my days locked away in my own personal tomb reminiscing only the good times, as my mind has shut down.

NICOL HOWARD

Take care of your Mind.

ABOUT THE AUTHOR

Nicol Howard.

Being a single mother living on a small estate in greater Manchester I have had my own fair share of mental health issues as well as seeing many people suffer at the hands of mental health. I have loved and sadly lost people due to mental health and have witnessed the impact their loss has left behind. I hope by writing this story and giving some insight into how my own mental health has made me feel, I can hopefully help people understand that this is a battle no person can or should fight alone.

Always Be kind and take care of your mind.

Printed in Great Britain
by Amazon